Surprised by Love

Ivy Marie

Ivy Marie Publishing

Contents

One

Anya

I STEPPED OUT OF my townhouse and tilted my face toward the sky, basking in the early morning warm June sun, made comfortable by a light breeze. Soon, the summer heat will come, and it'll be unbearable to be outside. I didn't have time to linger. I had to get to work. I hopped in my car and merged with the other early risers. Traffic was light for this beautiful Friday morning. Fridays are both my favourite and least favourite day of the week. On the one hand, it signifies the end of the workweek, while on the other, the day drags on as if it doesn't want the weekend to start.

I parked in the designated gated parking lot for Harrington and Sons employees, then made my way to the front door. I greeted the security guards as I passed, then took the elevators to the eighth floor. I greeted the handful of employees who were in a little earlier, just like me, to prep for the day. Sitting at my desk, I swapped out my flats for the pair of heels I keep in the bottom drawer, turned on my computer, and then went to the break room for coffee.

Settling back at my desk, I got to work. I reviewed today's schedule and prepared the client files. I left them on my assistant's desk for her to review. Before I knew it, the office officially opened, and the phone began to ring.

"Good morning." I greeted the first caller of the day. "You have reached divorce lawyer Bill Caldwell's office. How may I assist you?"

"I wish to confirm my appointment with Mr. Caldwell." The woman on the other end said. "It should be at ten am this morning."

I turned my attention to Bill's calendar. "Mrs. Davies?"

"Yes, that's right."

"I have you on Mr. Caldwell's for ten this morning."

"Good, good." She let out a sigh of relief. "Is there anything I need to bring?"

"Today is only a consultation. Mr. Caldwell will ask you some questions and collect some information so he can better assess your situation." I explained. "He'll also discuss with you the divorce proceedings. Of course, if you're uncomfortable with Mr. Caldwell, you are free to seek counsel elsewhere."

"Thank you. I look forward to meeting Mr. Caldwell."

I hung up and smiled at my assistant, who had settled into her desk across from mine. "Good morning, June."

"Morning, Anya."

"I put three files on your desk. Verify the information and greet the clients as they come in." I told her. "They will be your responsibility moving forward."

"Of course."

"Start with Mrs. Davies, she'll be here in less than an hour, and today is her first consultation."

She nodded and got to work. I fielded phone calls and confirmed or made appointments. Bill will be in court on Monday, so I reviewed and prepared the client's file. He will have to verify everything is in order, but I've been doing this long enough to know what he'll need. I took my lunch with the few friends I've made while working here. When I returned, June took her lunch, and I greeted Bill's last scheduled client for the day.

While Bill was with his final client, Steven from accounting stepped off the elevator. He looked nervous as he held a file folder. His eyes met mine, and he beelined it to my desk. Last time he looked this nervous, he had asked me on a date. This was something different.

"Hi, Steven." I smiled at him, trying to ease his nerves. "What are you doing up here?"

"I came across some inconsistencies for this department." He said in a hushed tone. "I wanted to bring it to your attention."

"You could have emailed me the report."

"I know." He smiled sheepishly. "But then I wouldn't have been able to see you if I did that."

I softened my smile from a professional one to a more personal and intimate one. "I appreciate it."

There was a moment between us where neither of us looked away. The elevator dinged, indicating a new arrival on this floor. Steven broke eye contact first, cleared his throat, and then handed me the file.

"Okay." I took the file from him. "What inconsistencies did you find?"

"The reports you have been sending don't correspond with what is actually in Mr. Caldwell's accounts."

I frowned, opening the file to see for myself. "I don't understand. How can that be?"

"The numbers don't lie." Steven came around my desk to point out the numbers to me. "The account is lower than it should be. It's subtle right now, so I haven't brought this to my boss's attention yet. If nothing changes, I'll have to report this."

"Thanks, Steven." I closed the file and stood. "I'll look into this and get back to you."

"Anya." He rubbed the back of his neck. "Do you want to grab a coffee after work?"

I stared into his kind brown eyes. Steven and I have been on a handful of coffee dates in the past few months. He's good-looking and nice. Any girl would be happy in a relationship with him. I'm not one of them. I tried, but it's just not working for me. If I'm going to have a man in my life, I want someone who will excite my nerve endings and make me feel like the most beautiful woman in the world. I'm not looking for love. I want more than what Steven offers.

"Sure." I agreed. "Coffee sounds nice."

"Great." He smiled brightly. "I'll come back up later to pick you up."

"Don't do that. I'll come down to your floor at the end of the day."

"Yeah, that makes more sense."

He kissed my cheek and rushed to the elevator. I watched him leave. June was watching us with a big grin on her face. I raised a brow, challenging her to comment on what had transpired.

"He likes you." June said, accepting the challenge.

"I'm aware." I acknowledged nonchalantly.

Her brows furrowed. "But you don't?"

"Steven is a nice man, there's nothing wrong with him." I closed my eyes and shook my head. "This is not a conversation we're going to have here at the office."

"Understood." June sobered, turning her attention back to her computer. "We can have drinks later, after your coffee date."

I shook my head. June and I have gotten close over the past three years since she became my assistant. We talk about plenty of things, including her love life, but mine has always been a taboo subject. I will not indulge her romantic whimsy. My personal life is just that, personal, especially in the love department.

Bill's final client left his office, signalling I could enter. Knocking on the open door to announce my presence, I entered and closed the door behind me. He didn't even look up from whatever he was doing. Something had his enraptured attention, and I didn't think it was any of his cases. Walking up to his desk, I dropped the file in front of him. Startling him enough to force him to look up at me.

"Anya." He looked back down at the file. "What is this?"

"You tell me." I rested my hip against the desk and crossed my arms.

"You dropped it on my desk. How am I supposed to know what's inside?"

I flipped it open. "Finances showing an inconsistency in your business account."

Bill gulped. "What kind of inconsistency?"

"The actual numbers are lower than the reports June submits to accounting."

"Then talk to your assistant." He pushed the file away. "Clearly, this is her mistake."

"Don't you dare blame June." I snapped. "I go over her impeccable work before it goes to accounting. This inconsistency can only be coming from you."

"That's impossible. Have accounting rerun the numbers. There must be a glitch." He sounded a little nervous.

"Bill."

I said his name with a disappointed tone. The man flinched and refused to look me in the eye. He knows the reason. I was not leaving this office without an answer. So, I changed tactics.

"Seven years, Bill." I said softly, uncrossing my arms and kneeling so we were at eye level. "I have been with you since the beginning. You can tell me the truth about what's going on. Why are you stealing company money?"

"Borrowed." He mumbled under his breath.

I didn't dignify that with an answer. Instead, I waited for a proper response. If he doesn't give me a suitable answer, I'll tell Steven to report him. Actually, I should report Bill to the CEO. When it appeared that I was never going to get an answer, I stood, taking a step back. He's made his choice.

Bill grabbed my hand in a panic, his eyes wide and pleading. "You have to help me."

I could hear the desperation in his voice. "What did you do?"

"Not here." He tugged me down and spoke in a conspiratory tone. "Seven o'clock. I'll pick you up at your place."

"Bill." I pulled my hand away and stepped back again.

"Black tie, Anya."

Reluctantly, I nodded my agreement. A moment of relief passed his features, quickly replaced by something else. Fear, maybe. Whatever I saw in Bill's face had me regretting my choice for tonight.

Two

Calvin

"Okay, next on the agenda is Janne's retirement." Wyatt flipped over the paper in front of him. "We'll need to find a new in-house lawyer."

"Did she not provide us with a suitable replacement?" Hector asked.

It was a valid question. Janne wouldn't leave us without vetting her replacement first. She's been with us since we moved from Hector's garage to the flourishing game company we are today. At our start, she was dating Wyatt's brother, which is how we'd all met, and she was studying to become a lawyer. CalTorAtt wouldn't have succeeded as well as it has without Janne's legal aide.

"She did. Janne suggested we reach out to Harrington and Sons." Wyatt replied. "Do either one of you have a different company that you'd like to reach out to?"

Hector and I exchanged a look. After years of being best friends, the three of us have mastered silent communication. Neither one of us would know what to look for in a new lawyer. We trust Janne completely.

"Nope." I answered.

"Okay." Wyatt made a note on his paper. "I'll set up a meeting with them and have Janne sit in on it."

"Is that everything?" Hector pushed away from the conference table.

"One more item." Wyatt looked at me. "Calvin, are you still having dinner with Marcel Wilson?"

I nodded. "I'm taking him to Velvet Table."

Hector whistled. "Fancy."

"I figured excellent food and good drink would open his mouth a little wider for the truths to spill out."

Hector burst out laughing, slapping the table to emphasize his amusement.

"Let's hope he's a good fit." Wyatt smirked, amused by my words but not as boisterous as Hector. "Our company could use one more investor for our new game to launch even more smoothly."

"Speaking of the game launch." Hector mused. "How is the gala going?"

"Everything should be going smoothly. I haven't heard from Miss Calhoon, so I'll reach out for an update." I said. "Invitations went out two weeks ago informing everyone of the location. RSVPS have been coming in. It's looking like everyone will show."

"Good." Wyatt nodded his approval. "Let us know if there's anything you need."

"One of you can wine and dine Marcel Wilson in my stead." I tried to pawn off my duty.

"I'm busy ensuring our new game is ready to launch in two weeks." Hector stood in a rush.

"I need to handle Janne's retirement and replacement." Wyatt said. "Besides, you're the face of CalTorAtt, and this falls under your role of responsibilities."

I grumbled. He's right. We created these roles at the very beginning. Wyatt handles all personnel and financial matters. Hector is a wizard with coding and works closely with the game developers and designers, while I manage the various client accounts and our public image. I am the face of the company—the man who does all the interviews. I don't mind, it's what I'm good at, but keeping up appearances can be taxing.

"If you had an assistant." Wyatt said softly.

I scowled at him. "Not after last time."

"It's nearly been a year, and we've recovered. I think it's about time you start looking into hiring someone new."

"I can handle the workload." I stood, ending the conversation. "I'm going home to freshen up."

I marched past Hector, who stood near the door, watching and listening to the exchange. It's not their fault. My last personal assistant weaved her way into my personal life. She not only broke my heart, but turned out to be a corporate spy who almost stole confidential information about our next game. I don't want another woman in my life—not at work, and especially not at home. They can't be trusted.

I arrived at the restaurant ahead of schedule. Punctuation is key, and being early helps to give power, or so my mentor taught me. The waiter led me to a curved booth along the outer wall. I ordered a drink, which arrived moments before Marcel graced me with his presence.

"Calvin Sinclair?" He confirmed.

I stood, extending my hand. "It's a pleasure to meet you, Mr. Wilson."

"I hope we'll be able to make a good business relationship." He smiled, taking my hand. "So, please, call me Marcel."

His grip on my hand was firm and confident. I gestured to the booth, and we both took a seat. It's only been a minute, and I already don't like the man. His smile didn't feel genuine. In fact, it felt rehearsed. His wavy blond hair was styled back, and his suit was professionally tailored. His eyes, though—those brown eyes—seemed too calculating.

"Why CalTorAtt?" I jumped right into the reason for this meeting.

"I'm an investor." Marcel began. "I keep my eye on smaller businesses and their profits. I offer to invest in companies I believe are going to become giants."

"So you believe that we'll be long-lasting and profitable? That's why you reached out to us?" I confirmed.

"Indeed. I take great pride in conducting thorough research before investing my money."

It's nice to hear that we've got the potential to become a giant game company, but coming from Marcel, it sounded unbelievable. CalTorAtt has been operating for twelve years. The first two years, it was only the three of us working out of a garage after university. I've been in this man's presence for five minutes, and I already want to run the other way. I get the sense that he's a slimy businessman, someone that CalTorAtt will not want any association with. The only way to know for sure is to play my part for the rest of the evening.

"I can see you don't believe me." Marcel chuckled. "You're not the first. When we're done with dinner, there's some place I want to take you."

I raised a curious brow. "Where is that?"

"It's a secret. Trust me, before the end of the night, we will be much closer."

I frowned, unsettled by his confidence with that statement. Throughout dinner, we discussed mundane topics. After our meal, which was paid for with the company card, Marcel had me follow him—by car—to a parking garage on the outskirts of Stramform downtown core.

"Here." Marcel handed me a simple black eye mask.

"What's this for?" I eyed it suspiciously.

"Wear the mask, Calvin. Everyone at this event is here for its anonymity."

Hesitantly, I took the mask. I really don't like the cloak-and-dagger stuff. It made me sick, reminding me too much of *her*. Marcel put a mask over his eyes and walked away. I looked back at my car, tempted to drive away, but I was a little curious as to where he was taking me. Putting the mask over my eyes, I caught up to Marcel.

He showed a guard something, then we entered the elevator he was guarding. The elevator only had one button—down. When the doors opened, I was surprised by the opulent lobby. Reds and golds decorated the walls and floor, from the ceiling chandeliers that hung evenly down a long hallway to the velvet on the walls. Everything looked rich.

"Evening, sir." A male receptionist greeted. "Do you intend to participate this evening?"

"Yes, along with my guest." Marcel said, pulling something out of his suit.

The receptionist typed on his computer. "I have you registered as number 32, and your guest is 33."

"Thank you." He turned to me. "Ready?"

"You haven't exactly explained anything to me." I countered, but followed anyway.

Marcel pushed through the doors at the end of the hall. "This is an auction."

It took my eyes a moment to register what I saw. A sea of suits floated around a massive room and converged around various platforms. On those platforms, young women, many appearing to be only girls, displayed artwork and furniture. It was overwhelming.

"Have a look around." Marcel encouraged. "Maybe something will catch your eye."

I began to move around the room, sensing Marcel trailing behind. Nothing on these platforms were of interest to me. A small commotion caught my attention. A woman, demanding to be let go, by someone who held her arm. I looked around. No one was stepping forward to help. Marcel looked on with interest, his eyes lit up, but he didn't make a move to help. I don't know what compelled me to step forward, but by the time I realized what I was doing, it was too late to back out.

Three

Anya

BILL WAS AT MY door at precisely a quarter to seven. I felt ridiculous leaving my apartment in a floor-length black dress with my boss. Bill opened the passenger side door for me of his Genesis, rushed to the other side of the Sedan and slid in behind the wheel.

Bill drove white knuckled to wherever he was taking me. He was clearly nervous. I wanted to ask him questions, but I didn't want to distract him from the road. He constantly looked in the mirrors as if he were expecting to be followed. I don't know what it was about tonight, but I had an ominous feeling that it would end poorly. Whether for me or Bill, I couldn't say.

Eventually, Bill pulled into a parking garage on the outskirts of Stramford's downtown core. It was close enough to get used, especially in the summer, but far enough that no one really wanted to walk from this garage to the core. So when I saw more than a couple of dozen cars parked on a higher level, I was genuinely surprised.

Bill parked among them, then reached over to pull out an eye mask from the glove box. "Here, you'll need to put this on."

"What is going on, Bill?" I demanded. "I want answers."

"I'll explain everything once we're there." He insisted. "Promise me you'll stay close."

I took the mask. "Okay, I promise."

Bill was off kilter. Usually, he's calm and in control while in the courtroom, but tonight he's on edge and scared. He helped me out of the car and tucked my hand in the crook of his elbow. He led me to a guarded door and showed the guard some ID or invitation. I wasn't sure which, and then we were let through into an elevator. I tightened my grip on Bill's arm, nervous with all the secrecy as the elevator took us down.

When the doors opened, I was awed by the opulence of the reds and golds that decorated the room. Bill walked up to the desk, showed the receptionist whatever he had shown the guard upstairs, and was given a number.

Bill put a hand on my back and led me down the hall and through another set of doors. The atmosphere in this room was different. I couldn't quite put a word to what I was feeling in the room, but it certainly wasn't a pleasant feeling. Bill took me around the room, which was decorated in darker royal blues with hints of silver. I saw paintings, furniture, jewelry, and other expensive things that I was certain collectors would pay a fortune for.

Bill stopped in front of a young girl wearing a gorgeous emerald-and-diamond necklace. The girl was shaking, her head held high so her eyes never came in contact with anyone. My heart went out to her, but I bit back any soothing words. I still don't understand why there's so much secrecy about the pieces in the room.

"This is what I've been buying."

"Jewelry?" I frowned, anger lacing my words. "You've been using company money on jewelry?"

"No." Bill whispered, signalling for me to lower my voice. "Look around, Anya, it's the girls who are on sale."

"The girls?" I said slowly.

I took another look around the room. Every item I passed was on display with a girl who looked to be between fifteen and eighteen years old. Most carried an edge of nervousness in their stiff shoulders, but a few seemed to bask in the attention of the men in the room. That's when I understood the strange atmosphere I felt when I walked into this room. Lust. These men were lusting after these children.

I turned back to my boss, unable to mask the disgust in my tone. "Bill!"

"Shh!" He warned, glancing around while tugging me away from the crowd. "That was Georgina, her sister asked me to save her."

"Her sister?"

"Yes. I bought her last time and helped her get home." Bill explained quietly. "It's been a few months, but now Georgina is making her debut. I have to win the auction to save her and keep my promise."

I looked back at the girl with the emerald necklace. Tall, thin, blonde hair and blue eyes, she was pretty and, in time, would be gorgeous. She was surrounded by men gawking at her. She was clearly going to be the popular one tonight. I looked at Bill. He was pleading with me with his eyes. I want to help save her. I want to save all these girls, but I don't know how to help.

"How did you get mixed up with this?" I asked.

"I was invited as a guest. I honestly thought I was buying a painting." He said with a scowl. "When the girl showed up at my front door, I was surprised. That's when I learned what was going on here."

"Why haven't you gone to the police?"

"There are high-ranking officials in this room."

I looked back at Georgina. "How can I help?"

Bill opened his mouth to reply when a big, burly man came up to us. "Sir, if you would come with me."

"Stay here." Bill told me. "I'll be right back."

I picked up a glass of champagne from a passing waiter's tray only to have something in my hand while I surveyed the room. How many of these girls was Bill able to save? I hope it was a lot of them if he is using company money. I tried to think of a way to help, but my mind was drawing a blank.

The men in this room should all be arrested. With the lustful way they were looking at the girls, there was no way they'd have innocent thoughts about what they'd do once the girl was purchased. A shiver ran down my spine at the thought of it. The champagne curdled in my stomach, and I had to breathe through my nose to settle it.

"Shouldn't you be up on one of these platforms?" One of the many men walked up next to me. "I'd pay a fortune to see a pretty jewel around your neck."

I didn't bother responding to him. Clearly, that wasn't my best course of action based on the growl rumbling from him. He gripped my arm, forcing me to face him.

"I'm talking to you."

He smelled of alcohol and cigarettes. I pitied the girl that he would buy. Unlike those defenceless girls, I can fight back. However, I'd have to be careful not to get kicked out.

"And I'm ignoring you." I tried to pull my arm out of his grip. "Let me go."

"You need to be taught a lesson." He tugged me forward.

"Unhand me." I ordered loudly enough to draw attention. "Or you will regret laying your hands on my person."

Someone from the sea of men stepped forward to be my rescuer. "The lady asked you to let her go."

"I am no damsel in distress." I replied, glaring at this new man.

He barely spared me a look, focusing instead on the man who still held my arm. Ridiculous. I could have freed myself in two simple moves—my heel on his foot, and my knee to his junk. The burly man from earlier, the one who took Bill away, came over. He looked at the man who was holding my arm, then at my arm, and then back at the man. He let me go as if I had the plague, and with a snarl, he stomped off.

"Miss, your companion has requested that I escort you to him." The burly man said.

I nodded, ignoring my would-be rescuer and followed the burly man. I downed my champagne flute, replacing it with another before we left the room. He led me down some halls to an area with closed doors. He opened one of them. As I walked in, I caught a glimpse of the plaque on the door that said 'Boss'. I had a bad feeling about this.

I stepped into the room, not sure what to expect.

Bill sat stiffly in a chair. Two men stood behind him with their hands clasped on his shoulders to keep him seated. He looked pale, but uninjured. My gaze drifted to the desk where a slender blonde in a navy blue pantsuit sat. Her legs dangled over the edge of the desk, her hands loosely holding the edge of the wooden piece of furniture. I was not expecting a woman to be the boss of this horrid place. Though it is also possible that she's a placeholder for the real boss.

The woman's pink lips curled upward in a calculating smile. "So, you're the secretary."

"Personal assistant." I corrected automatically.

"My apologies." She gestured to the free chair before her. "Please, sit."

I sat and crossed my ankles, trying to maintain an outward sense of calm. The burly man who brought me whispered something in the woman's ear. Her blue eyes darkened with anger. In that look, there was no doubt that she was indeed the boss, not a substitute.

"Deal with it." She ordered, then, in a blink, she was back to her more innocent look. "I apologize for the behaviour of our patrons. We will ensure it doesn't happen again."

"That is something you can not guarantee." I countered.

"As long as the patrons are in my house, I can ensure they conduct themselves accordingly." She smiled. "Of course, I have no control over what goes on outside this building."

I took a sip of champagne. "Before we get into the reason you brought me to your office, what shall I call you?"

"Miss Q."

"Then you may call me Miss A."

She threw her head back in a throaty laugh. "How did you end up as the personal assistant to this fool?"

"Behind every fool is a strong woman." I shrugged, instinct telling me that she responds to confidence and wordplay. "Wouldn't you agree?"

"Hey!" Bill protested.

"Hush." Miss Q warned. "I believe you and I will get along swimmingly, Miss A."

The woman smiled, studying me with her cool blue eyes. I gripped the champagne flute tightly. Warning bells screamed at me to run and never look back, except I can't do that. I'm a fool who likes a challenge. The adrenaline rush it brings when I succeed is thrilling. Miss Q, and this situation Bill has thrust me into, is a challenge I want to beat.

"What do you want from me, Miss Q?" I lifted the champagne to my lips.

She shifted to sit cross-legged on the desk. "What makes you think I want anything from you?"

"I'm in here, and not out there." I waved vaguely to the door behind me. "If you only wanted to see me, you would have done so from afar. This is private."

She rested her elbows on her knees and leaned forward, all business in her tone. "Are you aware of Bill's debts?"

"I am."

"I want my money, and Bill tells me you're the woman who can accommodate."

I shot Bill a glare before returning my focus to Miss Q. "Tell me how your operation works?"

"Excuse me?" Miss Q raised a delicate brow.

"Is this an open auction, or are the bids blind? Are the items purchased for a specified time or permanently owned?"

"This is an open auction." A devious smile pulled her lips up. "The purchaser owns the items auctioned. The length of time is dependent on how much is bid. All the terms are written in a contract and signed before the item is packaged and sent to the purchaser's house."

My ears perked up at the word contract. Those contracts may have a loophole that I could manipulate if I could get my hands on one. Miss Q will never let me have a look. So, how do I get one? The outline she provided wasn't much, but I was able to start to formulate a solution to help Bill and save Georgina. I don't like the idea.

"The emerald necklace." I hedged cautiously. "How much are you anticipating bringing in?"

Miss Q narrowed her eyes suspiciously. "Two hundred and fifty thousand."

I wanted to strangle Bill. He was already using company money, and there was no way he could afford tonight's little venture. I certainly do not have the funds to help him. I know someone who could help, and would if I asked, but I'm not going to involve him in this mess.

"Of course, there's also the hundred thousand he still owes me." Miss Q jerked her chin toward Bill.

"I have a proposition for you." I was already disgusted with the words that were coming out of my mouth, but I trudged forward anyway.

"What do you propose, Miss A?" Her eyes sparkled with intrigue.

"Put that necklace around my neck."

"Interesting, but my patrons may not appreciate a last-minute change."

"For two weeks, I'll ensure the necklace remains safe around my neck." I cocked my head, trying to sound more confident than I feel. "I'm sure your patrons would appreciate the personal guard for such a gorgeous piece of jewelry."

"Hmm." She mused. "Some may appreciate it."

"Whatever is brought in will cover Bill's debt."

She pursed her lips, contemplating.

"And cover the cost of the original owner." I added.

Miss Q smiled like the cat who caught the canary. "You have yourself a deal, Miss A. I do hope this auction is in your favour."

My stomach soured. I'm about to sell myself to the highest bidder. Who knew what horrors I would face while in the company of a stranger. As I was led out of the room, a thought occurred to me: what would happen if I didn't make the promised sum?

Four

Calvin

I STAYED IN BED longer than usual for a Saturday. Staring at the ceiling, trying to decide if last night was a dream or not. My buzzing alarm, though, wouldn't let me stay down for long. Slamming the off button, I forced myself to the shower. I'll never know if buying the hazel-eyed woman who goes by the name Anya was only a vivid dream or my reality by staying in my room.

Dressed, I made my way to the stairs. Can't start the day without a coffee. I took a peek at the spare room. The bed looked made, the lights were off, and I didn't see a suitcase. Tension rolled off my shoulders as they sagged in relief.

"Just a dream." I mumbled. "Yeah, there's no way a pretty face would sway me."

Satisfied, I proceeded down the stairs. That's when I heard it, a distinctly female voice coming from the kitchen. I froze. There's no way there's a woman in my inner sanctum. I vowed no one would enter here after *her*. Anya was just a dream. Created by something Marcel had slipped into my drink.

"It's only two weeks, June." Anya said.

I poked my head around the corner to see who she was talking to, ready to kick out the uninvited guest. But no one was there. Anya was talking on her phone. She looked comfortable at the dining table with her laptop open, phone to her ear, and her finger tracing around the rim of a coffee cup.

"You're my assistant, you can take over my job while I'm on vacation." She told the person on the other end. "I've sent you some notes, and you can always call if there's an emergency."

I stepped into the kitchen, announcing myself by getting a coffee. I put a pod into the single-cup machine, placed a mug underneath it, and hit the start button. Out of the corner of my eye, I saw Anya's shoulders tense. She was aware of me.

"Goodbye, June, enjoy your weekend." She hung up, then closed the laptop and turned to me. "Good morning, Calvin."

"Morning, Anya." I pulled my full cup of coffee from the machine. "Would you like another cup?"

"No, I'm good, thanks."

I leaned my hip against the counter and stared at her as an awkward silence fell between us. This whole situation and how we got here is unprecedented. I've never bought a human before, and Anya doesn't seem like someone who'd auction herself off on a daily basis. Though I could be wrong, I know nothing about this woman. Do I want to know more about her? I should know at least a little so that we can move forward.

"What now?" She asked quietly, eyes averted.

I blinked at her. "What do you mean?"

"Well, you bought me for two weeks. So, what do you want to do with me?"

"Nothing." I said quickly, and with so much indifference, it sounded cold to my ears.

"Excuse me?" Anya blinked those beautiful hazel eyes at me. "I don't understand."

I blew out a sigh and ran a hand over my face. "I don't know why I bought you. In the heat of the moment, I just knew that guy who was harassing you wasn't going to win the bid."

Anya tilted her head, assessing me. "Thank you."

"You're welcome." I mumbled, lowering my gaze to the cooling coffee in my hands. "What were you doing on that stage?"

"Saving lives."

I heard Anya stand. There was a hint of honeysuckle wafting off her as she neared. Sweet, warm, and soothing to the senses. I remember it from my childhood. Through my lashes, I tracked her from the kitchen table to the sink in the island where she began washing her mug. Done, she turned to face me, her arms protectively folded under her breasts as if she were hugging herself. It was a clear contrast to her bold demeanour when she stood up for herself last night. She was biting her lip as if contemplating her words very carefully.

"Calvin?"

I looked up. "Yes, Anya?"

"Can we not mention to anyone that we met at that auction?"

"Gladly." I agreed, not wanting the media to catch wind of this. "Maybe we met at a coffee shop."

"Neutral ground." Anya relaxed slightly. "One more request?"

"Depends on what it is."

"I can't stay cooped up for two weeks doing nothing, it'll drive me insane. Is there anything I can do to stay busy?"

I considered her request. Leaving her here by herself seems cruel while I'm busy at work all day. I also don't want to leave a stranger in my home unsupervised. Taking her to work will only draw suspicion. However, it might be the lesser of two evils. Maybe Wyatt and Hector can help me figure out what to do with her. Them I trust wholeheart-edly.

"What do you normally do for work?" I asked to buy myself time to think.

"I'm a personal assistant to a divorce lawyer." She answered.

"Personal assistant." I repeated. What are the chances? "I need a personal assistant."

Anya straightened. "You do?"

"Yeah."

"Then why do you not look happy about it?" She frowned.

"It's the logistics." I lied.

She nodded, her demeanour shifting as her mind got to work. I don't know how I noticed the change, but I did. It was subtle. I held back my amused smile lest she think I wouldn't mind having her around. There's no point in getting attached to Anya in any capacity. She'll be gone in two weeks.

"Right, me showing up as an assistant without going through the proper procedure would cause unwanted questions." Anya put a hand under her elbow and nibbled on the thumb of her raised arm. "A meet-cute at a coffee shop won't do. Would it be logical for your company to go through a temp agency?"

I considered her question. "I believe we do."

"We'll go with that."

"I don't follow."

"The temp agency. It'll explain my presence in your office."

I frowned at her.

"Anya, you don't even know what I do."

She blinked at me. "You, Calvin Sinclair, are the face of CalTorAtt, a company that made the popular match-3 game called Matchify. You started the company with two of your friends, Hector Barr and Wyatt

Henley. The three of you have worked hard to bring your company to the standing it is at now."

"I never told you my last name." I said, dumbstruck.

"You won't find anyone as good as me." Anya boasted.

"How did you find out my last name?"

"It's called the internet."

I've never looked myself up before. I don't know how easy it is to find information on me. "I'm going to work."

"It's Saturday."

I finished my coffee. "I have things to do."

"Then I'll go get dressed."

I belatedly noticed that she was still in her pyjamas—a pair of cotton pants and a tank top. My cheeks heated. She seemed so comfortable standing there in her pyjamas that I didn't even notice she wasn't properly dressed. Anya bounded out of the kitchen. To stop myself from staring at her retreating form, I busied myself with washing my mug.

Anya was back downstairs faster than any woman I know. I took in her attire: jeans, stiletto shoes, and an emerald top. The green from the top brought out flecks of green in her hazel eyes, making them even more mesmerizing. I clenched my jaw, lest it fall open. She is beautiful.

"I dressed based on what you're wearing." Anya said. "Is it all right?"

I cleared my suddenly dry throat. "It's fine, let's go."

I led her to the garage. I snagged the keys to the Bentley from the hook next to the door and unlocked the car. I started to get in when I realized I wasn't hearing Anya's heels clicking on the poured concrete. Looking back, I saw her staring at my motorcycle.

"Is this a Ninja H2SX?" She asked, awed.

"It is." I closed the Bentley door and went to her. "It's able to reach 300 km/h."

"998 cc supercharged engine with at least 200 horsepower." Anya rattled off, her eyes on the bike. "It has a hefty price tag for a two-seater. The H2R would be more fun to ride, but it's not street legal."

I had to pick my jaw up from the floor before speaking again. "I've never met a woman who knows bikes."

"It's not really the bike." Anya blushed a pretty shade of pink. "It's the speed."

"Still, most women prefer the Bentley or Ferrari."

"A Ferrari is good, but it can't beat the thrill of riding a motorcycle."

I locked up the Bentley and returned the keys. "Do you prefer the Ninja or the Ducati Panigale V4 R?"

"Tough choice." Anya's head moved between the two options. "Let's go V4. It may not be as powerful as the H2, but it's much more agile to take city corners. Long distance, though, I'd pick the Ninja."

"Excellent choice." I grabbed the keys and an extra helmet. "Safety first."

She took the helmet. I swung my leg over the bike, put on the helmet, and started the bike. Anya climbed on behind me and wrapped her arms around my chest. Every vehicle in my garage has a special sensor installed, so when they near the door, it'll go up, then close as I drive away—no need for a garage button.

Anya pressed into me as I sped along the streets. Without even needing to tell her, she leaned with me around the corners. The feel of her soft body against mine felt too good. I may have sworn off women because of the last one in my life, but I'm still a man, and Anya reminds me of that fact. Maybe having her around won't be that bad.

"That was fun." Anya said, removing her helmet.

"We can take the bike out any time you'd like." I offered.

She smiled at me. "I'd love that."

Her smile caught me off guard. It was filled with pure joy, lighting her eyes. She looked even more beautiful when she smiled, and my body took notice. These two weeks are going to be a real test of my control.

Five

Anya

I COULDN'T WIPE THE smile away. The rush of adrenaline the V4 provided gave me a kind of energy that's almost as good as great sex. Being able to ride a motorcycle, though, I'd prefer to drive one myself, will be the highlight of these two weeks with Calvin. I'm still not sure what to expect while with him. He says he doesn't want to do anything with me, unless he's gay, that will change.

There is no way Calvin Sinclair is one of those rare gentlemen. Sometime in the next two weeks, I can guarantee I will be in his bed. I have no doubt that sex is what those men at the auction are actually buying. Calvin won't be any different. At least, I don't think he'll be different. Today will be a good way to test him and gauge how honest he was this morning.

Calvin led me to his office, high on the twelfth floor. The elevator opened to a wide space occupied by a single curved reception desk. Which, at the moment, remained unoccupied. Behind that desk was a partial wall with a hall on either side. Calvin went down the right hall. We passed by open doors to unoccupied offices—two, to be exact. The name plates next to each door indicated they belonged to Wyatt and Hector.

"Is the office normally closed on the weekend?" I asked.

"Yes." He said, stepping into his office at the end of the hall.

"Yet, you're here."

"I have things to do."

I stopped in the doorway and stared. "I can see that."

Calvin had stepped over piles of files to get to his desk. "We have a gala in two weeks and I need to study."

"What about this mess?"

I didn't know where to step. Calvin looked at all the files as if he were seeing them for the first time. He then looked at me sheepishly.

"I, uh, pulled all those looking for these." He placed a hand on the files on his desk. "I then got to work on the gala and neglected to put them away."

"I'll make this my first project." I declared, picking up the closest file. "What is all of this anyway?"

"Information on every player on our platform." Calvin explained. "Their username, email, record of purchases, and whatever else they provided on their profile. I try to keep them updated, but I've fallen behind. It hasn't been an easy year."

"Do you not have an electronic system for all of this?"

"We do, and that's automatically kept updated."

I nodded. "Refile and update, got it."

"It's a lot, if all you have time to do is refile, that's fine." He said. "It'll at least keep you busy."

"I'll get it all done. Do you have a preference for organization?"

"I had it all by date. Whenever the user signed up, I made a folder and put it in the back."

"Inefficient." I mumbled.

Calvin obviously didn't hear me, or else he probably would have commented. Lacing my fingers together, I stretched my arms out and cracked my neck from side to side. I've got my work cut out for me.

I started by moving all the folders to one side of the room. Then I checked the wall of filing cabinets to make sure no file was left behind. Satisfied, I started to organize. This will be a two-step process. First, sort alphabetically, then alphabetically within that letter. I moved from the unorganized side of the room to the other as I made neat piles.

"Take your shoes off." Calvin growled. "The clicking is giving me a headache."

I scowled but obeyed. I kicked the shoes off toward Calvin's desk. The floor was cold beneath my bare feet, prompting me to move faster. This is how the day went. I organized, and Calvin studied the files on his desk. He paused to send out an email or make a call, then went right back to those files. By two, he was rubbing his eyes with the heel of his hands.

"Maybe you should stop for lunch." I suggested.

"Are you hungry?" His lips quirked upward.

"Yes."

"Do you like sushi?"

"I like anything as long as it's delicious." I shrugged. "I'm not overly picky."

He smiled. "Put your shoes back on, I'm done for the day."

I rushed to put the heels back on my feet, excited to get back on the motorcycle. Calvin took me to an authentic sushi restaurant. One with a conveyor belt running throughout, and the price varies by the colour of the plate taken from the belt. I've been here with friends, so I know it's delicious.

"I know one thing about you." I told Calvin after we were seated in a booth.

"What's that?"

"You have good taste in food."

He laughed. "Thank you."

I smiled. Calvin has a nice laugh, but I got the feeling he didn't use it often. It's only been a few hours, but I've noticed he's tense around me, and it's not because he bought me at that auction. If I had to guess, it's because of a woman who has hurt him in the past. Or, I'm the first woman he's had any form of relationship with who isn't his mom. My money would be on the former. There's no way a man as good-looking as him hasn't been on a date before.

As inconspicuously as I could, I studied Calvin. Golden highlights in his short, muddy hair stood out under the restaurant's fluorescent lights. Strong jaw, broad shoulders, he looked like he could protect his woman. He definitely turns heads as he walks the streets of Stramford, or anywhere else he goes. As appealing as all that is, it's his eyes that attract me the most—dark green eyes, as lush as a forest. I could get lost in those depths for hours. And they were so expressive.

"Anya, you're staring."

"Was I?" I looked away to take another plate of sushi from the conveyor belt.

"You were."

"Sorry. It's just, your eyes are breathtaking."

He stiffened, his voice cold. "Like emeralds, rich and beautiful?"

I reared back, obviously hitting a sore spot from his past. "No. They remind me of a lush forest, soothing to the soul and mesmerizing to look at."

"Sorry." Calvin looked down at his empty plate. "Let's make one thing clear. I'm not looking for any relationship to develop from my purchase last night."

"Okay." I agreed, a little flirting can test that flimsy lie.

"But I guess I can't keep you at arm's length while you're living in my house."

"Calvin, we can keep things casual, friendly." I reached out, lightly touching the back of his hand.

"No sex."

A smile flirted on my lips, and I batted my eyes playfully. "Only if you make the first move."

His blush was adorable. There was a flicker of interest in his eyes. It was so quick I could have imagined it. Just like that, I knew things would shift and he'll change his mind about not wanting sex, or anything else from me. I don't sleep with strangers anyway. Even if someone else bought me, I would have fought to keep my self-respect. Here and now, I can form that line in the sand.

"But I won't push the subject." I added seriously. "This is an odd situation for us both. So, my suggestion is that we take tomorrow to get to know each other so that we can at least call each other an acquaintance."

"Deal." He looked relieved by the suggestion.

Six

Calvin

I SHOULD NEVER HAVE agreed to get to know Anya better. Sure, we only talked about our likes and dislikes, but those simple things made her feel more human than the purchased item the auction implied she was. Not that I thought of Anya that way, but I could keep a wall between us much more easily. Now I like her. If I weren't so resolved not to let another woman in my life, I would spend my time forming a romantic relationship with her.

I parked under the CalTorAtt building on Monday morning. Anya got off the bike, but I couldn't move. Bringing her here on Saturday was fine. No one was around, but now everyone will see her. Questions will be asked, and rumours are bound to form. I wasn't ready to be the source of those rumours—again.

"It'll be okay." Anya prompted after removing her helmet. "Remember, I'm only a temp."

I nodded. No one needs to know that Anya and I came to work together on my bike. We just happened to arrive at the same time. I took her helmet and stored it with the V4. Without the helmet in her hands, the nerves eased slightly.

"It's been a year since I've had an assistant." I told her. "Wyatt and Hector will pry."

"I will follow your lead."

I took a deep breath and walked to the elevator. "You're from a temp agency, here to help organize while I focus on the gala."

Her smile felt like a reward. Suddenly, I wanted her to always smile, especially at me, exclusively for me. No one blinked an eye at Anya's presence in the elevator. By the time someone new entered the box, we had passed the main lobby. When she exited and followed me to my office, I heard the whispers starting—a ghostly sound in my ears. Everyone on my floor knows the tragedy of my last assistant.

Anya placed her purse by my desk and removed her heels before getting to work. She had made a decent dent in the unorganized files on Saturday, but there were still plenty to sort through. I turned on my computer and went through my emails. Reminders about interviews I have scheduled, and more RSVPs flooded my inbox. There was nothing from Miss Calhoon. I'll give her until this afternoon before I call.

It took longer than I expected for Wyatt and Hector to come and investigate the whispers about Anya. It was shortly after ten when Hector's low whistle alerted me to his presence. I looked up to find both of my friends in my office, their eyes trained on her.

"So it is true." Hector said. "You do have a woman in your office."

"Gentlemen." Anya greeted them as they both strolled further in.

"Who are you?" Wyatt narrowed his eyes at her.

"Anya Wright." She extended her hand. "It's a pleasure to meet you, Mr. Henley." She then turned to Hector. "Mr. Barr."

"Hector, please." He took her hand eagerly, kissing the back of it. "It's a pleasure to meet you, Anya."

She smiled pleasantly. I don't know why I felt a little jolt of satisfaction that she didn't smile at him the same way she did earlier at me. Wyatt took a seat. Questions were surely floating in his mind, but with the way he kept one weary eye on Anya, he wasn't sure if he should ask them now or later. Hector also took a seat, but he angled himself so he could watch her as she worked.

"How was your dinner with Marcel Wilson?" Wyatt asked.

Anya flinched at the name. Curious. I made a mental note to ask Anya about it later. For now, I kept my focus on my business partners.

"We will not be partnering with him." I declared.

"Why not?"

"He's not the right fit for CalTorAtt." I paused. "Anya, can you close the door?"

"Would you like me to leave?" She asked.

"No."

With a nod, she closed my office door before going back to work. I can't keep the truth about Anya from my two best friends. Besides, how Anya came to be in my life is in relation to Marcel.

"Hey, Anya." Hector interjected. "Why are you barefoot?"

"My heels give Mr. Sinclair a headache." She answered without pausing in her work.

"What are you doing?"

"Organizing." She glanced at me. "Shouldn't you return your focus to your business partner, Hector?"

He grinned. "My name sounds good from your lips."

"Don't go getting any ideas, Hector." I warned.

"Too late."

Wyatt snapped his fingers in Hector's face. "Focus. Why is Marcel Wilson not a good fit for our company?"

"I got a bad vibe from him during dinner." I explained. "But it's where he took me after that sinched it."

"Where was that?"

"An underground auction that sells women." I shook my head. "No, not women, but girls."

"Disgusting." Hector snarled, turning his full attention to the conversation. "Why would he do that?"

"I don't know. He claimed that we'll be much closer afterward." My gut sank. Marcel knows I bought Anya.

"I'll reach out to my brother, see if he knows anything about it." Wyatt said. "Something like that can not continue to exist."

"I'm willing to answer any question he may have." I took a deep breath. "Anya, Wyatt's brother is a detective. Would you be willing to talk to him?"

Her body stiffened, and she slowly turned to me. "Those girls need to be saved."

Wyatt frowned. "Why would Miss Wright know anything about this auction?"

"That's where we met." I said sheepishly.

Hector eyed Anya up and down with renewed interest. "Intriguing."

"What do you mean, that's where you met her?" Wyatt demanded, eyes narrowing at me.

I looked down, embarrassed about the truth, about what I'd done. Wyatt sucked in a sharp breath. I dared a glance up at him. My friend was staring at me wide-eyed and open-mouthed.

"You didn't." He breathed out.

I could only nod. My throat tightened, unable to verbalize the words.

"How much?"

"I used my own money." I defended, looking my friend in the eyes.

"I don't give a fuck about that, Calvin." Wyatt slammed a fist on my desk. "How much did you spend at an underground auction to buy a human being?"

I stared my friend down. There was no way I would ever admit how much I spent on Anya. The tension between us thickened to fill the room. No one said a thing, no one moved. I knew Wyatt would be pissed, but I thought Hector would have a say in this matter, too. He wasn't looking at me. Hector was looking at Anya with a thoughtful expression.

"How much is it for a night with you, Anya?" He asked.

"Hector!" I scolded.

"Oh, Hector." Anya purred, sauntering over to him. She trailed a finger down his cheek to his chin and lifted his face. "One night wouldn't be enough to satisfy you."

He hooked an arm around her waist and pulled her close. "How many nights do you think will be enough?"

"A big, strong man like you? I'd say a lifetime."

Hector threw his head back and laughed. "You and I are going to have so much fun."

She smiled at him. "As long as HR doesn't write us up."

He laughed again. "You heard her, Wyatt."

"What the fuck, Hector?" Wyatt sputtered. "You're okay with this?"

The song 9 to 5 started playing. Anya clicked her tongue, slipping from Hector's hold to fetch her phone. I could only stare. Was Anya's flirting legit? Was she attracted to Hector? I know many women swoon over him, but a tiny piece of me hoped she wouldn't be one of them. I'm not sure if I'm jealous of my friend or angry at myself for starting to like her.

"June." She answered with an exasperated sigh. "It hasn't even been one day."

Whatever her assistant said had Anya going pale. She gripped the edge of my desk as she swayed backward. I reached out and helped her to her feet. Slipping her shoes back on her feet, she rushed out of the room.

"Yeah, I'm still here, June." Anya said. "What is he doing out of his ivory tower?"

The door closed behind Anya, leaving me to fend off my business partners on my own.

"How long will Anya be around?" Hector asked, his eyes on the closed door.

"Two weeks." I answered.

"She'll liven up the place." He turned back around.

"You two are out of your mind." Wyatt stood, throwing his hands up and paced away. "How do you intend to explain her presence here?"

"A temp agency." I said.

"Out of the question. I refuse to falsify any paperwork for this whim of yours. What were you even thinking, buying her?"

"Why don't we say she's a friend, here to help?" Hector offered. He's always the mediator of Wyatt's anger.

"Whose friend? Yours?" Wyatt snipped.

"Of course. We get along wonderfully."

Wyatt studied both of us. With a growl, he sat back down heavily and crossed his arms. His lips pursed, and he glowered at us. Hector and I remained silent while Wyatt contemplated the situation. We can't move forward unless all three of us agree.

"You two better keep a close eye on her." Wyatt ordered. "I'll have my brother run a background check on Miss Wright so we don't have another Nicolette situation."

I winced at the reminder. I've been trying not to compare Anya to Nicolette.

Seven

Anya

"June." I said, answering my phone. "It hasn't even been a day."

"Mr. Harrington is here." She whispered.

I felt the blood drain from my face and had to grip the edge of Calvin's desk to stop myself from falling on my ass. He helped me up and steadied me as I put on my shoes. I rushed out of the room to have this phone call.

"Are you still there?" June hedged.

"Yeah, I'm still here, June." I said, recovering from the shock. "What is he doing out of his ivory tower?"

"Anya!" She scolded, scandalized.

I rolled my eyes, momentarily forgetting that she doesn't know I have a history with the CEO of Harrington and Sons. It is curious that he came down to Bill's office on the first day I'm officially on vacation. I took a seat in one of the six large, plush chairs that were set out behind the reception wall. The waiting area had one person sitting there with a file folder on his lap, looking very nervous.

"Tell me exactly what happened when he arrived." I ordered June.

"Well, Mr. Harrington looked at your desk with a scowl, then demanded to know where you were. I told him you were on vacation, then he stormed into Mr. Caldwell's office. I couldn't stop him."

"He just stormed in without checking if Bill had a client?"

June's voice was quiet when she answered. "Yes."

I rubbed my forehead. Bill better not breathe a word of my current predicament. Male voices could be heard through the phone. I knew those voices, one in particular very intimately.

"Hang up." I told June in a panic. "Hang up, now."

I don't know if she listened, because I pulled the phone away from my ear and hung up on my end as soon as the words were out of my mouth. I'm being ridiculous. At least that's what I told myself. Except that David Harrington has always been able to tell when I'm lying, even through the phone. This time when the phone rang, it wasn't June or David calling but Shane Williams. I debated ignoring the call. He's David's security, and both of our friend.

"Hello?" I answered cautiously.

"Anya, why aren't you at your desk?" David demanded.

I groaned. I should have known to ignore the call. "I'm on vacation."

"You never go on vacation."

"That's not true!"

"You've only ever taken time off for a long weekend." He stated. "I doubt you even know how to take a vacation."

"Are you calling me a workaholic?" I accused.

"I would never." He said, feigning hurt in his tone at the implication.

Hector and Wyatt exited Calvin's office. Clearly, their little meeting was over. Wyatt glared at me, but he caught sight of the man waiting, and he schooled his features to introduce himself. Apparently, the waiting man was there for an interview with Wyatt.

Hector placed a hand on my shoulder. "We'll talk later."

Instead of going into his office, Hector disappeared into the elevators. The distinct ding confirmed my assumption, since I can't see them from my spot.

"Who was that?" David asked accusingly.

"That was a new acquaintance of mine." I told him honestly. "Look, David, I'm quite busy relaxing and wish to get back to my vacation."

"We're not done. You're hiding something from me, and I will figure it out." He declared, then spoke in a softer tone. "I care about you, Anya."

"I know."

I hung up and returned to Calvin's office. He told me about the updated plan for explaining my presence at CalTorAtt. It could work, but I know nothing about Hector to even pass as an acquaintance. Hector's 'we'll talk later' was probably in reference to this.

I rubbed my stomach as it growled. I was trying to hold off on lunch so I could have it with Calvin, but I can't wait any longer. I looked over at him. He doesn't look like he'll stop anytime soon. Calvin leaned back in his chair.

"You don't have to wait for me to eat."

"You don't want to eat together?"

"I still have some work to finish up."

I hesitated. "We didn't bring lunch, so what's nearby?"

"Right." His cheeks tinted. "There's a cafeteria on the first floor if you want. I don't suggest leaving the building without me. Security will stop you from re-entering."

I collected my purse. "Do you want me to bring you something?"

He shook his head. With a shrug, to hide my disappointment, I left. I've never enjoyed eating by myself, especially in a communal space. In fact, I don't like doing much on my own. Coming out of the elevator, I looked both ways to orient myself. There was no indication as to where the cafeteria might be.

"Excuse me." I walked up to the front desk security. "I'm new here and was told there's a cafeteria."

The young man grinned at me. "The cafeteria is past the elevators. Trust me, you won't be able to miss it when you get far enough down the hall."

"Thank you."

I turned back to the elevators and continued past them through the hall I thought would have led to offices. Instead, as the security man stated, the hall opened into a large cafeteria. I took it all in. Employees filled the tables, engrossed in conversation, or continuing to work on their phones. No one paid me any mind. The cafeteria offered a wide range of selections, from Italian to Chinese to American, and every bite looked delicious. I selected penne pasta in a rose sauce, with a side of garlic bread, and water.

I paid, then went to find a seat. As I weaved through the tables, heads lifted to watch me. I felt like a museum curio by the way they stared. My eyes fell on an elderly man in a security uniform eating by himself.

"Excuse me." I stopped opposite him. "May I join you?"

"Of course." He gestured to the seat. "I don't recognize you. Are you new?"

"Sort of." I settled in and started to eat. "Mmm, this is good."

"How can you sort of be new?" His bushy brows knitted.

"I'm only here for a couple of weeks assisting Mr. Sinclair."

His eyes widened. "He hired someone after the last one?"

I frowned at him. "What do you mean by after the last one?"

"Never you mind." He mumbled.

I changed the subject as we continued to eat. I wanted to know more about the dynamics of this company, who I should avoid and who I should befriend. We talked without even knowing each other's names, as if we were old friends. This old man was easy to talk to, giving off a very grandpa-like aura.

"I best be returning to my post." He stated, pushing back his chair.

"My name is Anya, by the way." I said.

"Ben Riley." He offered his hand. "A little piece of advice, Miss Anya."

I shook it. "Go ahead."

"Keep your head down, rumours spread like wildfire, especially in the cafeteria."

I nodded. "Noted. If the timing works out, can I join you for lunch tomorrow? I'm sure you'll have more words of wisdom you can share."

He pondered the question. "I try to have my lunch around the same time every day."

I smiled, watching him as he left, using the opportunity to study the employees closest to me. I'm going to be the biggest rumour since, well, I don't actually know, maybe since Calvin's last assistant. I'll have to talk to Hector and compare notes on what he knows about what's going on in this company with what Ben has already told me. I have a feeling that Calvin doesn't actually know what goes on in the floors beneath him.

With a heavy sigh, I finished my lunch, cleaned up and returned to the twelfth floor. Wyatt was in the doorway, blocking my entry.

"Don't be late." Wyatt told Calvin. "This is an important meeting."

With that, he walked away without looking at me. He clearly doesn't like me, and I doubt that'll change in the two weeks that I'm here. I entered Calvin's office. He leaned back in his chair, rubbing his neck.

"Have you not eaten yet?" I asked, moving behind him to rub at his shoulders.

"No." He groaned. "God, that feels good."

"You need to eat."

His head lulled forward as I continued the message. After a minute, Calvin reached up and took my hand. He spun his chair to face me, keeping my hand in his. I didn't try to pull my hand back. I didn't want to. Calvin's touch sent little sparks of pleasure through my system. It's been a long time since any man had caused this kind of reaction in me.

"Odd question." He paused, uncertainly. "Do you know anything about Harrington and Sons?"

"That's where I work." I said tentatively. "Why?"

"I thought you said you work with a divorce lawyer."

"I do. Harrington and Sons has the best lawyers for all your needs." I told him, repeating the business's slogan. "They have divorce lawyers, family lawyers, criminal lawyers, and everything in between."

"We need an in-house lawyer. Do you have any suggestions on who we could hire?"

"That's a good question." I mused. "I can make a few calls and ask around."

"That's okay. Wyatt set up a meeting for tomorrow. I'm sure the names being brought in for consideration will be sufficient."

I went back to my sorting. Calvin doesn't seem to understand that for the next two weeks, I'm his assistant. Finding CalTorAtt the best in-house lawyer is part of the job description. Tonight I'll make a call. I think I know exactly who to ask for help from.

Eight

Calvin

I skipped breakfast and rushed Anya out of the house. I didn't want to be late for the meeting with Harrington and Sons. Anya kept pace with me as I marched from the elevator to the boardroom. Hector and Wyatt were already there. I looked at my watch, double-checking that I'm not late.

"What is she doing here?" Wyatt snarled.

"Anya will be an asset." I said, hoping it was true.

"I highly doubt that."

My fists clenched, getting angry on Anya's behalf. I understand what I've done isn't ideal, but he shouldn't be letting his frustration out on her. He should also understand that I don't want to leave her in my home unattended. This whole situation is complicated for all of us.

Hector raised his hands, palms out. "Anya can sit quietly in the corner and take notes."

"I'll go get a notepad." Anya said, then laid a hand on my arm and whispered in my ear. "You want Harlan Driscoll. No one else will do."

I nodded. It's going to be a long two weeks if Wyatt is going to be this bent out of shape about Anya being here. I settled into the chair next to Hector, with Wyatt on the other side of him, when the receptionist came to inform us that Mr. Harrington had arrived. Wyatt instructed her to let him in.

Mr. Harrington wasn't what I was expecting. I thought the CEO of Harrington and Sons was an older man. The man who entered the boardroom was young, blond, and good-looking. He introduced the intimidating man next to him as his personal security, Shane Williams. Wyatt, Hector and I introduced ourselves before we all sat down. Anya had slipped into the room behind them and, staying out of view of Mr. Harrington and Mr. Williams, took a seat in the corner.

"I reviewed the information you've sent me on the requirements you're looking for in a lawyer." Mr. Harrington began, opening the folio he brought. "These eight lawyers would best fit your needs."

He slid over the small stack of papers. Hector spread them out so we could see each one. My eyes scanned the top of each page. Harlan Driscoll wasn't among them. Could Anya have been wrong in her assessment? Or was this a test?

"Out of these eight, do you personally have a top three that you would suggest?" Wyatt asked.

"I had placed them in order of suitability." He replied, reaching over to tap at his top three.

"Harlan Driscoll isn't among your choices." I pointed out.

"Harlan is unable to be in-house." Mr. Harrington said.

"Is he not the best you have?"

His green eyes seemed to smile as his lips twitched. "He is."

I maintained eye contact. "Then why not include him? We could have at least decided whether he would be best for us or not."

"Calvin." Wyatt hissed. "What are you doing?"

"I'm simply inquiring as to why we're not being offered the best Harrington and Sons have at their disposal." I countered confidently.

"If you're not satisfied with who we've selected." Mr. Harrington stood and reached to collect the papers. "You're free to look elsewhere for a lawyer."

"Let us at least review who you've brought us." Wyatt rushed out, drawing the papers back to our side of the table. "You took the effort to conduct this search for us."

"Very well."

He tugged on his jacket, appearing ready to leave. Mr. Williams also stood. This is why we needed Janne here, but her father went into the hospital, so she left Stramford yesterday to be with her family. She would have been able to keep Mr. Harrington at the table longer and broker a better deal for us. She knows the language and what's best to look for in these candidates. I feel as though we fumbled, and Mr. Harrington wasn't impressed by our performance.

"Sit back down." Anya ordered. "We're not through here."

"Anya!" Mr. Williams spoke for the first time, his eyes going wide at the sight of her. "What are you doing here?"

Mr. Harrington only narrowed his eyes, his lips thinning, as he watched her move from her seat to our side of the table. I pushed my chair back enough so she could stand at the table between Hector and me. She crossed her arms, waiting for her order to be followed. Tension grew in the room until Mr. Harrington returned to his seat, followed by Mr. Williams.

"Harlan Driscoll." She said.

"Unavailable." Mr. Harrington answered.

"Lies."

"Truth."

"Anya." I wrapped my hand around her upper thigh and squeezed lightly. "What are you doing?"

Mr. Harrington's eyes zeroed in on my hand. "So this is how you spend your vacation, Peregrine? In the office of another man."

"David, what I do on my vacation is none of your business. The same applies to you, Shane." She stated, lowering herself onto my lap. "Refocus on Harlan."

The move was so casual on her part that it took me by surprise. My body stiffened—every damn inch of me. Anya shifted back ever so slightly, and I had to hold in a groan from escaping. I wrapped my arm around her waist to hold her in place. If she moved too much, I wouldn't be able to hide my hard cock if she shifted back any further.

"Harlan will be taking on a large project soon." Mr. Harrington said.

"Is the contract signed?"

He didn't answer. Anya had her phone in her hand and dialled. She put it on speaker phone for all to hear and placed it on the table.

"You've reached Harlan Driscoll's office." A female answered. "How may I assist you?"

"Trina, it's Anya."

"Harlan is expecting your call. Let me patch you through."

There was a beep, then a click before the music began to play. Within thirty seconds, the line was answered.

"Anya." A pleasant-sounding male voice rang out over the phone. "Trina told me you'd be calling with some exciting news."

"CalTorAtt is in need of a new lawyer. Would you be interested in the position, Harlan?" She asked him.

"Very much. I know their current lawyer, Janne Henley, we went to school together." He said proudly. "That fact alone tells me that CalTorAtt is a good company to be representing."

"Mr. Driscoll, this is Calvin Sinclair." I spoke up. "I'm one of the partners of CalTorAtt."

"Mr. Sinclair, I didn't realize this call was on speaker phone."

"Our apologies for not informing you. Anya says you're the best, and since you know Janne, that's a bonus. Why don't you send over a contract? We'd love to have you on our team."

"I would love to, honestly." Mr. Driscoll hesitated. "Unfortunately, Mr. Harrington wants me to represent HITGames."

Anya stiffened. "Drop them. I'll deal with David."

There was silence on the other end. "Mr. Sinclair, I have an availability today at one. May I swing by your office to meet you? I prefer to meet my clients face-to-face before contracts are signed."

"Of course." I answered. "I'll have Anya meet you in the lobby and bring you up to my office."

"Perfect, I will see you then."

Mr. Driscoll hung up. I may have been part of the conversation, but I don't understand what just happened. I looked at Mr. Harrington. He seemed almost relieved. What kind of power does Anya hold in this company?

"Peregrine, why don't you walk us out?" Mr. Harrington stood. "Gentlemen, I'll be in touch."

Anya slipped from my lap and exited the room.

"What the fuck just happened?" Wyatt snarled.

"That was hot." Hector whistled.

They both spoke at the same time, their words and tones blending. I put my hands together in the universal time-out symbol. My head spun as I tried to understand what had happened, including how strongly my body reacted to Anya on my lap. The softness of her curves burned my hand, and her honeysuckle scent permeated the air. It was intoxicating.

"Your little pet went too far." Wyatt ignored me. "I want her out of this building."

"No." I said, standing.

"No?" Wyatt stood to face me over Hector's head. "She just took over our meeting and was rude to Mr. Harrington."

"Anya got us the best lawyer to replace Janne." I countered.

"He wasn't part of the list."

"Mr. Harrington even admitted that Harlan Driscoll is the best. Did you not see his amusement when I asked about Mr. Driscoll?"

"We just poached him from HITGames." Wyatt reminded me. "How do you think they will react when they find out? You even said you didn't want to make waves with the launch so close."

"I will handle it."

"Will you? Or will you let your pet take over?"

My hands clenched. "Stop calling her a pet. Anya is a human being."

"That you bought."

"Enough." Hector stood, effectively becoming a human wall between us. "Look, I understand where both of you are coming from. Yes, Anya shouldn't have interrupted our meeting, but she also seems to have a connection to Harrington and Sons. If getting Harlan Driscoll is legit, I say we use her and whatever other connections she may have to our benefit."

"Fine." Wyatt huffed. "My brother will be in shortly to talk to you both about the auction."

Wyatt stormed out. Hector's shoulders slumped. I understand Wyatt's concerns and his worry. With the launch and Janne's retirement happening one on top of the other, we can't afford any mishaps or surprises. Anya is both. Poor Hector not only needs to ensure the game is ready to launch, but now he has to be the buffer between Wyatt and me.

"She's not like Nicolette." I mumbled. "She can't be."

Hector put a heavy hand on my shoulder. "It'll all work out. By the way, what was all that during the meeting?"

"Anya works for Harrington and Sons. I didn't know about her connection to Mr. Harrington. That was a surprise to me, too."

"We should be grateful she's on our side." He laughed. "I have a feeling she's a force to be reckoned with."

I nodded. Hector began to leave when I remembered something.

"Can you bring an old laptop to my office?" I asked.

"Why?"

"Anya's going to transcribe the electronic information of our users into my paper files."

"I'll create a profile for her in our system."

"Thanks."

I stared down at the seat I had occupied during the meeting. Why did she sit on my lap? Anya could have remained standing. What was with Mr. Harrington calling her Peregrine? I can't seem to figure her out. Was she using me for some jealousy game between her and Mr. Harrington? I hope not.

The way my body reacted to her on my lap was cumbersome. Maybe it's because I haven't been with a woman for over a year, and now one is living with me for two weeks. Yeah, that's it. My stiff cock has nothing to do with Anya and her sweet honeysuckle scent, or her soft, curvy body pressing against me twice a day. I've just deprived myself of a woman's company, and Anya's femininity is hard to ignore.

Nine

Anya

I WALKED DAVID AND Shane to the elevator. None of us spoke a word until the doors closed, sealing the three of us inside.

"What the fuck is going on, Anya?" Shane exploded. "Friday, you're in the office, then over the weekend, you send an email about taking a vacation. Not a future vacation, but one starting immediately on Monday. This isn't like you."

"Are you looking for a new job?" David asked calmly.

"No." I answered. "Something happened on the weekend that forced my hand."

"Will you tell me about it?"

I had no intention of letting David or Shane know what kind of situation I had found myself in. It'll only draw attention to Bill and his thievery, even if it was for a noble cause. The elevator stopped to let people on, which halted our conversation. The box emptied its occupants on the min floor.

David took my hand and tugged me to the front entrance. Leaning my body back, I tried to pull free from his hold. Shane placed his hands on my back, pushing me forward. No fair. They knew I wouldn't be able to break free from them both when they teamed up like this. I also didn't want to go past the security desk, Calvin warned me I might not be able to get back in.

"David, let me go." I said calmly, not wanting to draw too much attention. "I'm not leaving you."

Close to the door, David spun, dropping my hand and cupping my face. "Are you in any danger?"

"No."

I didn't even hesitate. I'm in no danger with Calvin. David stared at me, eyes searching mine for any lie. The man is like a human lie detector when it comes to me. I've never been able to get away with a lie, not even in our youth. He kissed me, lingering a little longer than he should have for being my ex, then rested his forehead against mine.

"I don't like not knowing." David said. "Especially when it comes to you, Anya."

"I'll be back in the office before long." I removed his hands from my face. "Trust me."

"I do." He said. "Always have."

David stepped back, turned, and strode out of the building. Shane patted me on the head, like he does with his kid sister, and followed his friend and boss out. As they left, a plain-clothed cop walked in. I knew he was a cop from the badge on his hip. He waved to the security and entered the elevator. I, on the other hand, was stopped, and they had to call up to Calvin's office to confirm my identity.

"Anya." Calvin gestured me forward. "This is Detective Cameron Henley, Wyatt's brother. Cameron, this is Anya Wright."

"Ah, so you're the woman my brother told me about." He said in a way of greeting. "I'd like to talk to you first about this underground auction."

I shifted uncomfortably on my feet. "Sure."

"Let's use Calvin's office. We don't want to draw too much attention." He turned to Calvin. "Can you give us the room? I'll text you when we're done."

Calvin looked at me worriedly, but Detective Henley crossed his arms and waited. This was apparently non-negotiable. With Calvin out of the office and the door closed, Detective Henley gestured to the two chairs in front of Calvin's desk. He could have chosen the table in the room, but clearly wanted to make me comfortable as he interrogated me.

"I am here in an official capacity." Detective Henley said. "But I'm also here as a favour to my brother."

"How does that work?" I asked.

"Officially, we know about the underground auction, but it's too exclusive to sneak in an undercover cop. So with yours and Calvin's statement, we might actually be able to start an official investigation." He explained. "Unofficially, I want to make sure you won't cause any trouble for my brother and this company."

I nodded, understanding his intentions. "Well, unofficially, an acquaintance of mine asked for help with their debt and insisted on showing me where the money was going in person. That's how I ended up at the auction. My acquaintance has been buying the girls sold at this auction and helping them get home. That night, it was going to be the last one because of the debt incurred."

"Okay, now what's the official story?" He asked, pen primed to his notepad.

"This past Friday, I discovered my boss was syphoning company money, so I confronted him."

"Your boss at Harrington and Sons?"

I narrowed my eyes at him. "Did you do a background check on me?"

"It's part of my job, Miss Wright. Now, back to your boss, what's his name?"

"Bill Caldwell." I said through gritted teeth.

Detective Henley wrote down the name. "What did he say when you confronted him?"

"He said he borrowed the money and asked for my help. He wouldn't tell me a thing while in the office, but said he'd pick me up later that night and to dress for black tie."

"Where did he take you?"

"A parking garage, if you show me a map, I can point out the exact one." I elaborated. "Bill had me put on an eye mask, then he took me to an elevator—which is guarded by the way—showed the guard something, then the elevator took us down. I was not expecting opulence when the doors opened."

"This is where the auction took place?"

"That was only the reception area. Down the hall and through a set of doors is where I learned what was going on. Girls between the ages of fifteen and eighteen were on display with items that were for official sale. I was the only female in the room." I shivered at the memory. "It was disgusting."

Detective Henley curled his lip in agreement. "How did you get sold?"

"I put myself up on that stage."

His pen froze. "Why would you do that?"

"Bill was taken away by security. After some time, security came to fetch me. The auction's boss wanted their money back, and Bill told them I could do it. I made a deal that Bill's debt would be cleared, and the fee for the girl he was going to buy would be covered by me going on that stage."

Detective Henley stared at me wide-eyed. "You met the owner of the auction?"

"I did, she goes by the name Miss Q. I also had her explain how the sale is processed."

"Please, go on." He had his head down, ready to write.

"The purchaser owns the items auctioned for a period of time, depending on the bid. So you can imagine the bids are quite high." I paused. "You should ask Calvin about this because all terms are written in a contract and signed before the item is sent to the purchaser's house. If I could get my hands on a contract, I was hoping to find a loophole."

"You kept saying item, why is that?"

"The girls were never mentioned. It's the item they have that you'll probably find in the contracts. Miss Q was cautious in her wording, as if she was conscious that anyone at any time could be wearing a wire."

"Is there anything else you can think of that could help?"

I shook my head. "I don't think so."

He handed me a card. "Call or text if anything comes to mind. Now, unofficially, what are your intentions with CalTorAtt?"

"Nothing. Calvin has me for another ten days, then I'll be back to work at Harrington and Sons."

"What about your brother?"

I glared at him. "If my brother were ever to reach out, I wouldn't help him. I hope your background check revealed that my father had disinherited me and I have no connection to the family."

"What if your father reinstated your inheritance?"

"I don't need or want it. The second he cut ties with me, so did the rest of the family." I stood. "If you're done questioning me, Detective, you can turn your attention to Calvin."

"I didn't mean to offend." He said calmly. "I'm only trying to protect my brother, his friend, and this company after what happened last time."

There it was again. Ben had mentioned it at lunch yesterday. Something clearly happened in this company that has affected more than just Calvin. My gut told me that I needed to find out what it is.

Ten

Calvin

"DONE." ANYA ANNOUNCED.

I looked up from my phone to stare at Anya. She stood proudly in the center of my office, hands on her hips, and not a single file remained on the floor. It took me a minute to register that all the files were put away.

"The files." I said dumbly.

"They are sorted alphabetically and put away." She walked over to one of the many filing cabinets. "I've labelled the drawers so you know where to look. And, this empty drawer is for your investment files."

She tapped the closed drawer closest to me with her knuckle. That only took her four days. If she's just quickly matching electronic records to paper and vice versa, she'll be done in no time and have nothing to do for the remainder of her time here.

"That's the only job I have for you." I said.

She rubbed the back of her neck. "I know. Now, if you'll excuse me, I'm going to take a break and meet up with Ben."

"Ben? Who is Ben?" My pulse jumped, thinking that someone else in the company was attracted to her.

"One of the security guards in the main lobby." Anya slipped her shoes on, grabbed her purse and headed for the door. "I'll be in the cafeteria if you need me."

"Anya, my love, marry me." I heard Hector from the hall.

She laughed. "When all the stars burn out, I'll be yours."

"You wound me."

"I know where to get a nurse outfit."

Hector's laugh echoed from the hall until I saw the man at my door. "God, I love that woman."

I didn't say anything. The image of Anya in a nurse's outfit flooded my mind. No doubt that'll be in my dreams tonight. Unfortunately, Hector's face is drawing out a dark jealousy within my gut. Anya is so casual with him, yet she keeps a professional barrier between us. Granted, I asked for it on day one. But she's grown on me. Every day with Anya, I'm finding myself liking her more and more. And Cameron's positive report he sent last night from his interview with her, and the niggling worry of her being anything like Nicolette has nearly vanished.

"Did you read Cam's report?" Hector asked.

"Twice." I held up two fingers.

"Should we go see how Wyatt's taking the news?"

"Lead the way."

I followed Hector over to Wyatt's office next door. He rapped on the door once before entering. Wyatt was on the phone, and based on the one-sided conversation, I assumed it was with his brother. It was childish, but I wanted to rub the report in his face, proving that Anya is no threat to us.

"There has to be something." Wyatt gritted out. "Anything."

Hector and I took seats, waiting.

He ran a hand over his face. "Yeah, I haven't forgotten our parents' anniversary. Hector and Calvin are here. I'll see you tonight, Cam."

"So?" Hector prompted. "What did Cam have to say?"

"He likes Miss Wright and doesn't believe she's anything like Nicolette." Wyatt answered. "As much as I want to hate her, I find it increasingly hard to do so. I trust Cam's opinion."

"Cameron's report swayed you that much?" I asked curiously.

"When you had your time with Cam the other day, she came to see me."

My gut twisted. "Why'd she do that?"

Wyatt shook his head. "Details don't matter. Anya has a backbone and appears very honest. Cam's report proves she told him the truth, and there are no red flags in her background that we need to worry ourselves with. At least that's what Cam said, of course, he won't show me her background check."

Hector grinned. "You called her Anya, not Miss Wright."

Wyatt glared. "That's her name."

Now I was curious as to the conversation between Wyatt and Anya. I want to know how Anya changed my friend's stubborn mind about her. Whatever it was makes one thing about her very clear: Anya Wright is an amazing woman.

"Update?"

Hector snapped his fingers in front of my face. "We lost you for a minute. Where did you go?"

"Nowhere." I swatted his hand away.

"I was asking if you had an update from Miss Calhoon?" Wyatt asked. "The gala is only a week away."

"I've reached out but haven't heard back. I meant to follow up again, but things have been hectic." My phone began to ring. "This is Calvin Sinclair."

"Calvin." Miss Calhoon said with a dreamy note in her tone. "I was following up with the venue, and there's a problem."

"What kind of problem?"

"The manager double-booked the space."

"You never booked the space to begin with." An irritated voice said in the background.

"If you could come to the venue, we can discuss alternate solutions."

"Stay there, I'm on my way." I rubbed my forehead.

"What's the problem?" Wyatt narrowed his eyes.

"I'll fix it."

"Take Anya. I don't want her wandering around the building alone."

"I'll babysit." Hector said eagerly, shooting his hand up in the air.

"No need." I said, gritting my teeth.

My friend's eagerness to be with Anya rubbed me the wrong way. I stormed out of the office, heading down to the cafeteria. I scanned the vast space for Anya, acutely aware of the room's volume dropping. Her head was bent, but I'd recognize her raven black hair anywhere. She was sitting next to an older man with grey hair and dressed in a security uniform. That had to be Ben. My earlier unease about him was let out with a sigh of relief.

"Your grandchildren are adorable." I heard her say when I was close enough. "You'll have to tell me all about them next time."

I stopped at the table. Anya didn't look up right away. Ben did, his eyes going wide at the sight of me. I know being in the cafeteria is out of character for me, but I came for Anya. She finally looked up, the sunlight from the wall of windows catching blue undertones in her hair, and smiled. Arms I didn't realize I'd crossed, unfolded and hung by my side. That smile of hers is a weapon. Something inside me snapped, breaking my control.

"What a rare occurrence to see you out in the wild, Mr. Sinclair." She teased.

"Break's over, we have some place to be." I held out my hand, helping her up. "And it's Calvin to you."

"As you wish, Calvin."

I tugged her close. Her hand still in mine, I placed it on her lower back and held her against me. Lowering my lips to her ear, I whispered. "I like my name on your lips."

She sucked in a breath as a blush rose to her cheeks, but I didn't have the luxury to enjoy it. I tugged her out of the cafeteria and back to the elevator. In the silence and isolation of the steel box, I realized what I said and where I said it. Embarrassment had me ducking my head. Anya squeezed my hand, wrapping herself around my arm.

"Calvin." Anya whispered.

I lifted my head to look down at her. "Anya."

"I'll say your name as many times as you'd like."

My eyes widened at her. Was she flirting or teasing? I couldn't tell. The elevator doors opened. I was paralyzed trying to figure her out. I just crossed a line I told myself I wouldn't cross. Anya tugged me off the elevator before the doors closed on us.

"Where are you taking me?" She asked.

"The Sunset Palace."

Anya stumbled. Despite still holding her hand, I reached out and caught her around the waist with my free arm. I shouldn't have, she felt good in my hold.

"You don't have to spend even more money on me."

My cheeks flared as I realized what she meant. "No, that's where the gala is held."

"Ah."

The way Anya said that one word, I thought she might have been disappointed. But why? I pondered that all the way to the hotel. I wanted to keep talking to Anya and explain the call I had from Miss Calhoon, but the helmets didn't have a two-way communicator. Until now, I had no need. I always rode my bikes solo.

She didn't say anything when we arrived at the hotel. I didn't want to leave the helmets with the bike, so we carried them inside. The doors to The Sunset Palace were manned, and the doorman welcomed us with a kind, non-judgmental smile. Anya took the helmets and headed straight to the front desk, where they were placed in a room behind it.

I called Miss Calhoon. "I'm here, where would I find you?"

"The main ballroom. I can come to the lobby." She answered.

"Stay there." I hung up and focused on Anya, who returned to me. "The gala is a week away. I want your honest opinion on everything."

She nodded with an air of professionalism in her posture and followed me to the ballroom. Miss Calhoon, a petite brunette, was arguing with a grey-haired man in a tweed suit. When she noticed me, she turned her full attention to me.

"Calvin." She practically sighed in relief. "As I said on the phone, the hotel double-booked this room."

"We did not double-book." The man ground out as if he was tired of repeating himself. "As I've said many times, you never booked with us."

"So, we'll need to find an alternative location for your gala." She continued, ignoring him.

"Calvin Sinclair." I extended my hand in greeting.

"Mr. Jorge, hotel manager." He said, eyes widening slightly at my name.

"Do you have any space we can use for a gala next Friday? There will be anywhere from 150 to 200 guests attending."

He pursed his lips. "There is another room more suitable for that many guests."

I gestured for him to lead the way. Mr. Jorge took us to the second floor. The room was considerably smaller without the opulence of the ballroom. I couldn't picture how this room could transform into a worthy space. That'll be for Miss Calhoon's event team to figure out.

"This space can host 300 guests." Mr. Jorge explained. "There's a small kitchen through those doors on the left and bathrooms through the far doors."

"Is this room equipped for a projector to be set up?" I asked.

"Yes."

I pulled out a credit card. "Put the deposit on this card. CalTorAtt will use this room for the gala."

"Of course, Mr. Sinclair."

He took the card and left, not before shooting Miss Calhoon a smug look. Anya's heels were muffled on the carpeted flooring as she explored the space. I turned to Miss Calhoon, needing to ensure the room won't affect the final results.

"Miss Calhoon." I began.

"Iris, please." She said with a purr to her voice. "Now that the room has changed, we will need to work diligently to create a new design concept."

"Yes, you will. You are the event planner. A grave error such as this should have never occurred, Miss Calhoon."

"You are absolutely right." She pulled a tablet from her purse and leaned into me. "The original concept won't work. We don't have the space. We can keep the tables, but it might be a little cramped for waiters to walk around serving food."

I watched as Miss Calhoon scaled down the original ballroom design. She rearranged things, trying to keep everything that had been previously agreed upon. It didn't look right.

"Something has to go." I said.

"It's a gala, Calvin." Miss Calhoon smiled at me. "Extravagant is a must."

I took a step back from her, very uncomfortable with her nearness. "Anya, can you have a look at this?"

"This room has good acoustics." Anya said, returning to me from the other side of the room. "You should have no problem projecting your voice for your presentation. I would suggest you still use a mic at a lower volume so no other noise overlaps with your voice."

"There will be a sound system set up." Miss Calhoon said.

I took the tablet from Miss Calhoon and showed it to Anya. She studied it with a frown. "That looks crowded. What time is this gala starting?"

"Seven." I said. "There will be a catered dinner, then I'll make my presentation, and after maybe some light dancing."

"That's rather late for a heavy meal." Anya's frown deepened, her eyes scanning the room. "If I were planning this, I'd set up an open bar and have hors d'oeuvres served throughout the night. Cocktail tables can be scattered around so that guests have places to gather and set down their drinks. I like the idea of dancing, but maybe have it before the presentation."

"That won't be possible." Miss Calhoon stated.

"The décor should be simple and elegant." Anya continued as if Miss Calhoon never spoke. "This gala is for the investors, CalTorAtt should be thanking them, not flaunting their success."

"I'm the event planner, let me handle the gala." Miss Calhoon sneered. "Who are you anyway?"

"Anya Wright, I'm-."

"My girlfriend." I cut Anya off.

To her credit, she didn't even blink at my proclamation. Instead, Anya smiled, wrapped an arm around my waist and placed a hand on my chest. Every time Anya presses her body against me, all my blood rushes south. I put my hand on her hip, holding her to me and handed the tablet back. The proclamation was rash, but I don't want Miss Calhoon's flirtatious attention.

Miss Calhoon looked shocked, then bristled at Anya's changes. "I know what this gala needs."

"I prefer Anya's suggestions." I said firmly. "I want a new design sent to me by tomorrow for approval."

"The catering is already set." She countered.

"Can you not make the necessary changes?"

Miss Calhoon winced. "Not on such short notice."

"I will give you the weekend to figure it out. If by Monday you are unsuccessful, then I will no longer be in need of your services."

I guided Anya to the door. Mr. Jorge stood there, for who knew how long. With a nod of approval, he handed me my credit card. Anya fetched our helmets, and the realization of my actions curdled my gut. I had practically fired Miss Calhoon with only a week until the gala. What the fuck am I going to do? No, the better question is—what the fuck was I thinking?

Eleven

Anya

A THRILL WENT THROUGH me when Calvin called me his girlfriend. It wasn't real. I knew that. Miss Calhoon was too overt in her flirtations and didn't pick up on Calvin's discomfort. He used me to reject her. What was really surprising was that he was using my suggestion for the gala so readily.

I played the part of girlfriend until we got outside. "So, I'm your girlfriend now?"

Calvin sucked in a breath, a red hue creeping up his cheeks to his ears, and he ducked his head. "I'm sorry, Anya."

I scowled at him. A man being vulnerable is endearing, but this lack of confidence and constant apologizing is frustrating. The moments where he's bold, like today in the cafeteria and just now in front of Miss Calhoon, were incredibly sexy. I want more of that version of Calvin to shine through.

"Are we going back to the office?" I asked, a little bite to my tone, as I put on the helmet.

"Yeah." He said slowly. "I won't cross the line again."

I wanted to rip my helmet off and yell at him, but he started the engine, cutting off all communication. Damn it. If this is how it's going to be for the next week, then I might need to collect my vibrator. If he'd never shown me this confidence, however fleeting, I could have lasted another week. My body is dying for release, and my fingers may not be enough tonight. The vibrations from the bike's motor didn't help any. It only wound me tighter. We may have agreed to keep things casual.

Hector was in his office when Calvin and I returned to CalTorAtt. Instead of continuing down the hall with Calvin, I stepped into Hector's office. He looked up from whatever he was doing and smiled.

"Anya, what a pleasure." Hector greeted me.

"Anya?" Calvin questioned.

I closed the door on Calvin, flipping the lock for extra measure. I need to question Hector without any interruption.

"Uh-oh." Hector said. "What's wrong?"

"I can't take it anymore." I turned and walked over to Hector. "The tension is palpable."

Hector came around the desk. "Just to confirm, it's the sexual tension you're talking about."

"Yes."

"There's a simple solution." He grinned at me. "A romp in the sack to alleviate all that coiling need."

Hector waggled his eyebrows, and I laughed, patting his chest. "As desperate as I am, it won't be with you, Hector."

He placed his hand over mine, holding it to his chest. "I'm always here if Calvin doesn't man up. Fingers, cock, mouth, whatever you need."

"There's a piece of the puzzle I'm missing." I took a seat, and so did Hector. "After the first few hours with Calvin, I got the impression he's been hurt by women in the past, and it makes him hesitant to move forward. So, I suggested a casual, friendly relationship. There have been moments when he's bold and confident, then he'd duck his head, ashamed of what he did or said and apologize."

Hector sighed, running a hand over his face. "Calvin was hurt by a woman. I think he may have been in love with her, but she turned out to be a corporate spy. All their time together was just an act on her part."

"Oh." My heart went out to the man.

"The simple fact that he flirted with you is a step forward for him."

I sat there for a moment, absorbing this new information, when it clicked. "Was Calvin's last personal assistant the woman who broke his heart?"

Hector stared at me. "How did you know that?"

"Never mind that." I waved him off. "But I understand now."

"What do you understand?"

"That I'm going to need my vibrator." I stood and kissed his cheek. "I won't hurt Calvin."

"Anya?" He turned in his seat as I headed for the door. "What are you going to do about Calvin?"

"Nothing."

I will tamp down the lust and keep things professional. Calvin doesn't need another flirtatious assistant to spark rumours. Nor does he need a fling, or another broken heart. Calvin needs a friend and a confidence boost. I can do that. Though if Calvin changes the terms we set, I won't say no.

Twelve

Calvin

I LEANED BACK IN my chair and watched as Anya worked on the laptop Hector had provided. This woman is giving me whiplash. On day one, she was cautious but friendly, and as we got to know each other, she warmed up and flirted lightly. But, as of yesterday, and her talk with Hector, she's turned frosty. Not mean, only carefully controlled neutrality. It bugged me. I like her flirting. Maybe she doesn't want me flirting with her, at least I think that's what I was doing.

It hasn't even been 24 hours, and I already miss her smiles. She wouldn't even get on the Ducati this morning and insisted we take the Bentley. I've opened and closed my mouth several times this morning to ask her what was wrong, but the words kept getting stuck in my throat. I didn't want her to say that I was the cause of her demeanour today.

Fuck it. I don't need to ask her. I can ask Hector.

"I have an errand to run." I announced.

"Do you need me to join you?" Anya asked without looking up.

"No, you can stay here."

I left my office determined to get answers. Hector wasn't in his office, which meant he would be down in development with the rest of his team. I went down two floors. Sure enough, Hector was at a computer typing furiously, along with the rest of the team. No one noticed that I even arrived. I placed a hand on his shoulder, making him jump.

"Calvin! What are you doing here?" Hector turned to face me.

"We need to talk."

"Okay?"

"Not here." I looked around. "Somewhere more private."

Hector laughed. "They are too focused on combing through the new game. Less than a week before this thing launches."

"Still, I don't want anyone to overhear."

"Okay, come step into my secondary office."

Hector led me to another room. This one held a foosball table, a ping-pong table, a vending machine, and bean bag chairs. He locked the door behind us and sank into a bean bag. Hector patted the one next to him. I cringed but settled down. Actually, I sank down deep with an oof.

"Okay, what is this about?" Hector asked seriously.

"What did you and Anya talk about yesterday?"

"That is between friends."

I struggled to turn in the seat to face my friend. "She changed."

Hector frowned. "Changed how?"

"She's." I hesitated, trying to find the right way to describe Anya's shift. "Colder, as if she's distancing herself from me."

Hector groaned, throwing his head back and running a hand over his face. So their talk did have something to do with her change.

"What?" I pressed.

"She doesn't want to hurt you." Hector said, partially muffled by his hand still over his mouth.

"What are you talking about?"

Hector stood effortlessly from the bean bag. "Anya knows that you fell in love with your last assistant and were hurt when she turned out to be a corporate spy."

Anger and embarrassment warred within. "And how did she find out about Nicolette, Hector?"

"I only told her that you got badly hurt from your last relationship." He put his hands up defensively. "She pieced together the assistant part. Nicolette's name was never brought up. I don't know if she knows it."

I struggled to get up. Hector reached out and helped haul me to my feet. He was fighting back a smile, but my glare nipped it in the butt.

"Anya's parting words to me yesterday were that she won't hurt you." Hector said. "I asked her what she was going to do, and she said nothing. As in nothing is the word that came out of her mouth."

I turned, walking away from my friend, trying to sort through what he said with Anya's actions. She doesn't want to hurt me. I think I understand what she's trying to do, and that is what's hurting me. My chest tightened. Anya doesn't want to remind me of Nicolette by flirting like Nicolette, then leaving.

I ran my hands through my hair, tugging at the strands as my mind raced. Spending time with Anya this week had me forgetting all about the pain Nicolette caused. I think I'm ready to move forward. No. I am ready to move forward. Anya is who I want to move forward with, despite the contract and the time constraint.

"Thanks, Hector."

I rushed out of the game room, or rather the chill room as he likes to call it, and returned to my office. Wyatt was exiting my office. He gave me a strange look, but I ignored it. I marched over to Anya and closed the laptop lid.

"Hey!" She looked up at me. "What did you do that for?"

"We're going out for lunch."

"I'm having lunch with Ben."

I picked up the landline on my desk, used for internal calls only and called down to security. "Ben?"

"Speaking." The elderly man answered.

"This is Calvin Sinclair. I'm taking Anya out for lunch."

The man chuckled. "You treat her well, she's a sweet girl."

"I'm glad we understand each other." I hung up and stared at Anya. "Let's go."

Anya didn't say a word. From the office to the Bentley, to the restaurant, she remained quiet. When she tastes the food, she'll moan in delight, which will loosen her lips. This lunch will change everything.

I got out of the car, coming around to open the door for Anya, but she was already out before I even made it halfway. Waiting for her at the hood, I put a hand on her back to guide her to the front of the restaurant. She arched her back away from my touch, but I didn't lower my hand.

"You're going to love the food here." I promised.

"This could have waited." She said. "You'd have me for dinner."

An image of her on my bed with my head between her thighs flashed in my head. I held in a groan at the mental scene. I need her to start talking to me before I can even consider getting her to my bed.

I pulled the door open, ushering her inside. A pleasant-looking woman greeted us as we walked in. The diner was busy, but it didn't deter me. With menus in hand, the hostess led us to a booth for two and said the waitress would be by shortly. Anya looked around, her eyebrow raising before she picked up the menu. I waited for her to say something.

"The Greasy Spoon." She said mildly. "How did a billionaire like you discover a diner like this?"

"I wasn't always a billionaire." I said blandly, picking up the menu. "I recommend a hamburger. They are the best you'll ever have."

"That's a bold statement."

"If I'm wrong, you can call me a liar."

Her lips twitched. Finally, a hint of her true self. I almost sagged in relief. Almost. She still sat stiffly in the booth. Victory will only come once she relaxes.

A curvy waitress sauntered up to our table. "Well, well, well, if it isn't my two favourite customers."

"Hi, Darlene." Anya smiled up at the woman. "How's life?"

"Oh, the usual. My back aches, my children never stop complaining, and my husband still loves me." She replied, then with her pen gestured between us. "Are you two on a date?"

"No."

"Yes." I said at the same as Anya.

Both women looked at me, but I kept my focus on Anya. Her eyes widened as she seemed to register something in my face, then a blush crept up her cheeks, and she looked down. Darlene chuckled low, which only caused Anya's head to duck even lower.

"Shall I ring up the usual for you two, or would you like something else?" Darlene inquired.

I waited for Anya to take the lead on that question.

"Yes, please." She answered softly. "With sweet potato fries."

"Sure thing." Darlene wrote it down, then shifted to me. "How about you, sweetness?"

"The usual is fine, thank you, Darlene."

"Coming right up." She collected the menus. "It won't take long for your shakes."

"So you're a regular?" I teased Anya lightly. "What's your usual?"

"The Big A with onion rings." She lifted her gaze tentatively. "Is this really a date?"

"Yes, Anya, I want to learn even more about you."

"Why? Only one more week and our paths won't cross again."

I frowned at her. "Is that what you want? Is that why you've suddenly decided to distance yourself from me?"

She flushed. "I don't want to hurt you."

"Hurt me? How could you hurt me?"

"I probably remind you of her in some way. The woman you had a relationship with last."

Darlene returned with two milkshakes in frosted mugs, with their respective shaker holding the extra beverage that couldn't fit in the mugs. She put them down on the table before moving on to other patrons. Anya reached for the mug, rolling it between her hands, and refused to look at me. This won't do. I took a deep breath, letting it out slowly while pushing the milkshake aside.

"Her name was Nicolette." I began, feeling my throat tighten at the recollection. "She was my assistant for a year before she betrayed me."

"Calvin, you don't have to." Anya said softly, finally looking at me.

I reached for her hand. "I can't, no, I won't let that bad relationship stop me from moving forward."

She nodded, pushed her milkshake aside, and gave me her full attention.

"Nicolette seemed perfect. She was professional and efficient. She completed tasks before I even thought of having her do them. In many ways, you remind me of her." I took in a shaky breath and lowered my gaze to our hands. I focused on the feel of Anya's soft skin under my thumb as it rubbed back and forth before continuing to speak. "Nicolette's flirting boosted my ego. Eventually, the flirting morphed into kisses, which later led to her being in my bed, and a relationship began to form. Deep in my subconscious, I knew it wasn't a real relationship because there were things I never told her."

"What happened?" She asked.

"Hector and Wyatt were wary of her and tried to warn me to be careful. I wouldn't listen. I was too wrapped up in Nicolette that it almost ruined our friendship." I looked up to meet Anya's hazel eyes to find concern swirling in their depths. "One night, I woke up to go to the bathroom and found my bed empty. I caught her on my laptop, stealing information on CalTorAtt's newest game. We were going to announce it very soon. I could have handled that, her being a corporate spy."

Anya squeezed my hand. "You haven't told Hector or Wyatt this part, have you?"

I shook my head. "Not only was Nicolette working for our rival at HITGames, she was dating someone there, too. While she worked on the laptop, she was on the phone speaking in the same bedroom voice she used on me. I heard her say that sleeping with me was only a job, that her heart belonged to him, and that even under normal circumstances, all I have is my looks."

"That's not true." Anya said firmly, pulling away when our food arrived. "You are hardworking and loyal to your friends and company. I've been watching you all week, Calvin. There is still plenty I don't know about you, and that's fine, but I do know that you don't care about your looks. As a member of the female population, I will admit that you are good-looking, and yes, it caught my attention, but that's not why I started flirting with you."

"It's not?"

"Well, actually, that first day when you took me to the sushi restaurant, I flirted because I wanted to test you. See if you were lying about not wanting to sleep with me." She admitted. "As I got to know you, and you relaxed around me, I did start to flirt more earnestly. When Hector told me you were hurt by your last relationship, I made up my mind that I didn't want to hurt you by reminding you of her. Our time is short, so I decided to keep things professional."

I laughed. "Ironically, your decision is what pushed me to bring you here for a date. I like it when you flirt, Anya, it's like a balm to my self-confidence."

Anya smiled before digging into her hamburger. It wasn't quite the brilliant smile that I long to see, but it's a start.

Thirteen

Anya

NICOLETTE RAINES IS A bitch, partially because of what she did to Calvin, but also because it's her personality. As soon as he said that Nicolette was dating someone from HITGames, I knew exactly who he was talking about. Throughout middle school and high school, Nicolette reigned as Queen Bee Bitch. She's not just dating someone from HITGames. She's engaged to marry the company's CEO—my brother.

Damn it. Even though I have been disinherited and am estranged from my family, they still seem to meddle in my life. If anyone at CalTorAtt learn about my brother at HITGames, they'll think I was another corporate spy, elaborately placed on the inside. I have two options. Confess everything now, or pray my familial connection will never surface.

"Tell me about yourself." Calvin restarted the conversation after we'd dug into our meal.

"What do you want to know?" I asked, hoping he would steer clear of the topic of family.

"What drew you to apply at Harrington and Sons?"

"I didn't apply."

He furrowed his brows. "Then how did you get a job there?"

"David. We grew up next door to each other. Went to the same private school and attended the same social gatherings that our parents forced us to attend. Dated each other." I put my burger down and reached for the milkshakes. I left it open to tell him about my family. Except, I can't bring myself to do it. "I almost got trapped in that life of wealth and luxury."

"What do you mean?"

"I was helping David pack for university when I remembered the going-away gift I had for him was still sitting in my room. I rushed home to retrieve it. That's when I overheard our mothers planning our wedding. When I told David, he asked me if being married would be so bad, then he kissed me to prove his point."

Calvin sucked in a sharp breath. "You're not engaged, are you?"

I shook my head. "David was very convincing that day. Instead of going to university myself, I would stay, be the perfect little future wife, and wait for his return. I was giddy with the prospect of being his wife."

"What happened?"

"After a year of attending social events and paving the way for David's return, I started to get bored and lonely. Attending those stuffy gatherings filled with fake people was only tolerable when David was at my side." I munched on my sweet potato fries. "I convinced my father to allow me to attend college. I told him that by furthering my education, I'll be able to be more useful to David than being a simple trophy wife. Our families could become even more powerful."

"That worked?" He asked incredulously.

"Power, money, and image are the three things my father cares most about." I let a small smile play on my lips. "College was a reality check.

I discovered life outside the country clubs, fancy clothes, and names that seemed to matter. I started to rebel against my father, much to his chagrin, by working part-time jobs that were below my station."

"So, during college, you shifted from entitled rich girl to normal, everyday student." Calvin teased. "What happened when David returned home from his time in university?"

"I didn't think I was entitled." I countered. "But I did own the title of snooty little rich girl."

"Snooty, entitled, there's not much difference between the two."

"I only wanted the best quality of everything, but I knew money had to be earned, not given." I retorted. "Now, when David returned, his father immediately put him to work in the company."

"He didn't go to you first?" He asked, amazed.

"He had Shane track me down. They had become friends while in university. Mr. Harrington was not happy I'd shown up at his company after all those years away from high society. He also knew I was disinherited from my family fortune and practically exiled."

"What a minute." Calvin put up a hand to stop me. "You skipped over some important information."

"Did I?"

"Disinherited and exiled." He repeated.

I shrugged. "It's because of my rebellion. Because I had a part-time job, I was bringing in money and living my life for myself. I refused to go back to the guilded cage, so my father put his foot down."

Calvin looked disgusted. At first, I was horrified and shaken by what my father had done. He had given me an ultimatum—marry David when he returns, and my rebellion will be forgiven or lose everything I've ever known for the life I was choosing to live at that moment. I chose my freedom. The friend I had gained in college, Kelsie, helped me through the transition.

"It took Shane nearly a year to find me."

"Why so long?"

I grinned. "I was travelling with friends for a while, then found a job in a small town as a receptionist for the mayor. When Shane found me, I was more than happy to leave. The mayor was getting handsy."

"Okay. So, you're back in Stramford, seeing David for the first time in years. Did he hire you on the spot?"

"Basically, yes. Even after learning about my disinheritance and the argument he had with his father, David wanted me around. He was officially the CEO at this point and could do whatever he wanted. He tried to rekindle what we had, but there were no embers left between us, so he shifted gears and strengthened our friendship. I worked as David's personal assistant for five years before asking to be transferred to another department. I was tired of people saying I was only in the position because I was sleeping with the boss. Despite how well I did my job, no one seemed to believe I could actually do it until I transferred and kept the same level of quality."

Calvin winced. "That must have been tough."

I shrugged. "David and Shane were always there for me, and always will be."

"You and Shane are friends because of David?"

"Yes, he treats me like a sister, nothing more." I pointed a fry at him. "Your turn. Tell me how you came to own CalTorAtt."

"It's not as interesting as your story."

"Doesn't matter. You know my past, it's only fair that I learn about yours."

Fourteen

Calvin

I OPENED MY MOUTH to answer, but instead requested the bill from Darlene. Her timing in coming to collect our empty plates was impeccable. Anya sipped on her remaining milkshake, eyeing me expectantly. It's not that I don't want to answer her, I will.

First, I need to show her the beginning. It's nerve-racking. Aside from Wyatt and Hector, no one knows about my past, not even Nicolette. My past, my origin, is not for any tabloid to expose and exploit. I don't want sympathy or to be looked down upon. My private life is just that—private. Anya is different, I can sense it deep in my bones. I want her to know everything.

My silence, though, didn't gain me any brownie points. Her lips pursed when I paid the bill, her arms crossed when she got into the Bentley, and she angled herself away from me. She was mad, maybe even embarrassed. She told me her story, was vulnerable with me, and I shut her down when the tables were turned.

I let her stew as I drove to the poor, rundown neighbourhood that I grew up in. The various mayors of Stramford have abandoned this part of the city. The only reason it hasn't been bulldozed is so that those of low income, or even less, have a place to go that doesn't ruin the image that the mayors have tried to maintain over the years.

"You're a jerk." Anya spat out, shifting to glare directly at me.

"Anya." I said plaintively.

"Don't Anya me. You wanted this to be a date, and so far it's been terribly one-sided. You've plied me with delicious food and got me to reveal my past. Then, when it's time to reveal your past, you shut down."

"Anya."

"You know, I thought that there could have been something starting between us." She continued her rant. "But I can see now how mistaken I was. Maybe it'll be best if we maintain distance until the contract is up."

"Anya." I said sternly.

"What?" She barked back.

"Look around."

She pulled her glare from me and looked out the windshield. I heard her breath catch. We were in my old neighbourhood. Long trailer park homes lined the roads, the grass was brown, yet there were still children who played catch in the postage-stamp yards. The citizens watched the Bentley wearily as it drove slowly through the area. Not that I blame them. Rich folk don't usually come here unless they have an agenda.

"Where are we?" She asked softly.

I stopped the car in front of a pale yellow home. "This is where I grew up."

Anya looked at me, then back out of the window. Starting life here and becoming who I am now is impressive in itself and hard to believe. The yellow home was raised on cement blocks. Some siding was missing. Whoever lived there now maintained the honeysuckles my mom had planted years ago in an attempt to make it more inviting.

"My dad left when I was five, which forced my mom to find a job. She ultimately needed two jobs to put me in school." I explained. "She always said that the visual of her success in life would be me, but I'd need an education to succeed. School was tough. I didn't have many clothes, and no one wanted to be my friend, but I worked hard. I wanted to make my mom proud. In turn, she made sure I had everything I needed."

Anya's hazel gaze softened when she looked back at me. I couldn't quite read her expression, pity, maybe, or possibly compassion. Whatever it was, I couldn't handle it and refocused on the road to take her to the next stop down memory lane. She rested her hand on my wrist and squeezed lightly. I took my hand off the steering wheel to lace my fingers with hers. The contact was grounding. The next neighbourhood I wanted to show her was for middle-class people. A stark difference from where we just came from. The houses were larger and the yards pristine. There was life and hope in this neighbourhood.

"This is the area where Wyatt and Hector grew up." I told her. "When we met in middle school, the three of us just clicked, there's no other way to describe it. They saw me alone at recess, sat down beside me, exchanged names, and that's how it started. Even their parents welcomed me and Mom into their homes."

"How long until you three decide to start a gaming company?" She asked. "Was it always the dream, or something you grew into?"

"Hector was always fiddling with a computer and playing with code. Toward the end of high school, we discussed creating the game that Hector was designing. The world now knows it as Matchify. It was only a rough concept at the time. We needed further education to make it a reality. Together we researched other companies, the various roles within the company, and then what sort of education we'd need after high school."

Anya smiled. "Hector must have been thrilled when he was finally able to make his game concept a reality."

"He was." I agreed. "Only Hector and Wyatt could afford University, so I sought out part-time jobs. I worked as a janitor, or in the mailroom, then moved up to coffee boy in a couple of different companies so I could get a feel for how they operated."

"Smart."

My lips quirked upward at the memory as I drove us back home. "I was moving up in the business world and surprised myself by how much I was enjoying it. When Hector and Wyatt returned, we immediately got to work on the game and our company all in the comfort of a garage. One of the men I was working for, at the time, took such a liking to me that he provided start-up funds."

"That's amazing." Anya said with genuine amazement in her tone.

"We got CalTorAtt up and running sooner than we expected. Through everything, I always had my mom's support. With my part-time job, I was able to move us both out of the trailer park and into a low-income apartment. She still worked so she could help with the bills. It wasn't necessary, but she wanted to do it."

"Your mom sounds like a wonderful woman."

"She was." I swallowed hard.

"Was?"

"She passed away almost two years ago now. Cancer."

"Calvin." She said softly. "I'm sorry. I can't even imagine the pain."

I could only nod. It still hurts to talk about her. Anya didn't say anything as if she sensed that I needed the quiet. Eventually, I parked the Bentley in my garage and shut off the engine. I closed my eyes, feeling tears prickling, on the verge of escape and rested my head on the headrest. Anya pulled her hand from mine and got out. The loss of her touch hit me soul deep. Mixed with the pain I was already feeling, I found it hard to breathe. I was startled when she opened my door.

Anya took my face in her hands. "From what you told me, I can confidently say that your mom was immensely proud of you until her last breath."

A smile fluttered on my lips. I needed to hear that. I rested my forehead against hers. Wrapping my hands around her wrists and letting my thumbs rub on the inside. I needed the intimate touch. I needed Anya. Comparing my short time with Anya and my long time with Nicolette, I can confidently say they are polar opposites. Where Anya is warm and sympathetic, Nicolette would have been condescending and indifferent. The more I learn and compare, the more I question what I ever saw in Nicolette.

"Thank you." I said quietly. "Aside from Wyatt and Hector, no one knows of my past."

"I'm honoured." She said honestly.

We stayed like that, forehead to forehead, for a long moment. I shifted, letting go of one wrist, to unlatch the seatbelt. Anya stepped back so I could get out, but I didn't want her to move away from me. As I stepped out, I simultaneously cupped her head in my free hand and pressed my lips to hers.

She froze, stunned by the action. When she didn't kiss me back, I feared I overstepped or maybe read the signs wrong. I let her go, slowly, my pounding heart hoping she'll pull me back in.

"Do that again." Anya ordered breathlessly.

I stared at her, hesitating in case my mind conjured those words. Anya fisted the front of my shirt, hauling me back to her, wrapped an arm around my neck and kissed me. This was real. I wrapped Anya in my arms and kissed her back fervently. Anya tasted sweet as ice cream, though that could have been from the milkshake she had at The Greasy Spoon. I wanted her to taste this sweet all the time.

She let go of my shirt and repositioned my hands to her ass. I squeezed, growling possessively as I pressed her closer. Anya wrapped her legs around me, losing her heels in the process, and opened her mouth so I could get a better taste. Our tongues clashed in a desperate need for more.

"Anya." I growled. "Not here."

"Then take me inside." She placed kisses along my jaw and down my neck, blurring my vision.

I carried Anya into the house but halted at the base of the stairs. "I don't have any condoms."

Anya pulled back quickly. I could see her mind spinning in the depths of those green-flaked hazel eyes as she processed what I'd said. If she said no, I was putting her down and racing out to grab a box. That single kiss ignited a fire in my soul. I needed to have Anya like I needed air. Nicolette had nothing on this woman. I almost groaned at the thought of my ex, but then Anya smiled wickedly, and only thoughts of the woman in my arms were my focus.

"Mouth and fingers." She decided. "You can buy condoms later."

With the decision made, I continued upstairs to my bedroom. Closing the door behind us, I placed her on the ground. We worked on undressing, then came back together like magnets. Lips never parting, I walked her backwards to the bed, helped her to lie on top as I crawled over her.

My pulse pounded in my ears as I trailed kisses down to her breast, where I took the nipple greedily. My hand played with the other breast, my fingers mimicking what my mouth was doing. Licking, nibbling, rolling and pinching the nipple, drawing out cries of bliss from Anya's lips. Moving my mouth to the other breast, I slid a hand down her flat abdomen to her sweet heaven.

I groaned. "You're so wet."

I ran a finger along her seam before inserting a finger. She gasped and spread her legs further apart. I slipped a second finger inside, and I watched the pleasure on her face as my hand fucked her. My mouth watered for a taste.

"Calvin." Anya moaned. "More. Give me more."

Eyes connecting with mine, she pushed at my head to go further down her body. I chuckled against her skin, obliging. I sucked on her clit, eliciting a cry. Her hips jerked upward, and her legs spread even wider. I held her leg open for a better angle. Anya surprised me by wrapping her hands behind her knees and holding her legs open as wide as they could go.

I groaned. With tongue and fingers, I fucked Anya senseless. She writhed at my attention, her body tensing as her orgasm rose. Unable to hold back, Anya's orgasm peaked, and my name was on her lips with a cry. I lapped at the juices greedily. My cock ached. I wanted to be inside her and feel those walls squeezing me. I had to hold back until I could buy those damned condoms.

I brought my mouth back to hers, three fingers now inside her, and with my thumb paying attention to her clit. Anya let her legs fall free and wrapped her arms around me. I rested my other hand on her waist, needing to have as much of me as possible touching her.

Her nails clawed my back when the next orgasm rocked her. I stayed still until she relaxed before pulling away. I returned to Anya with a washcloth and cleaned between her legs. My erection jutting out proudly. Anya licked her lips, her eyes locked onto my cock.

"Your turn." She said, shifting to her knees.

"It's okay, you don't have to." I assured her.

"I want to."

Before I could protest further, Anya wrapped her hands and mouth around my cock. She hummed, and god damn stars bloomed behind my eyes. With a growl, I placed a hand on the back of her head as she bobbed back and forth. I moved my hips in time with her rhythm. She shifted her hands to play with my balls and took me deeper.

"Anya." I growled. "I won't last much longer."

In response, she hummed happily and hollowed her cheeks. I cursed, my hand fisting her hair as my hips bucked forward. I warned her. Anya had shifted a hand back to my cock, anticipating this. I ejaculated, and she swallowed it all.

Pulling back, she smiled wickedly. "Don't you feel better now?"

"I'd feel better inside you." I admitted, bringing her lips to mind for a bruising kiss. "Tomorrow, you're not wearing a stitch of clothing, so I can fuck you any time the need arises."

"After you buy condoms."

"There will be a box in every room."

Her eyes lit up at the prospect. "Promises, promises."

Fifteen

Anya

My body was deliciously sore this morning. I didn't expect Calvin to be so...assertive and carnal. He's exactly what I've been craving in a man. If I'm not careful, I could fall in love with Calvin Sinclair. He already has my body wrapped around his, literally and figuratively. My heart doesn't need to be his either.

Calvin came downstairs in grey sweatpants. My mouth watered at the sight of him. He was well-toned, not overly muscled, and his muddy red hair stood up at odd angles. I itched to run my fingers through his hair and kiss him. Except that will lead to more sex, and as exciting as that'll be, my body needs a little longer than a few hours' rest.

"You're dressed." He said, sounding disappointed.

"I am."

He came around the island, wrapped his arms around me from behind and rested his chin on my shoulder. "Why?"

"Because I am."

"Mmm." He kissed my neck. "I can change that."

"Yes, you could." I agreed when the toaster popped. "Butter that toast and put down two more slices."

He pulled away, and I slid the omelette I was making onto a plate. I handed it to him, then turned to make my own breakfast. Once made, I joined Calvin at the table.

"This is really good." Calvin complimented after a bite. "How did you make it so fluffy?"

I grinned. "It's a secret."

He practically hoovered the plate of food as if he hadn't eaten in twenty-four hours. A pizza was the last thing we ate, taking a break from sex to talk. It made yesterday even more special. I ate my breakfast more slowly.

"Anya." Calvin pushed his empty plate away. "About yesterday. Um, I want to make sure we're on the same page."

"Same page?" I asked casually while collecting our plates.

"You agree that yesterday was only sex, right?" He cleared his throat. "I hope you understand that I'm still not looking for any form of a bonding relationship."

My heart tightened. I'm not looking for a relationship either, but it was still hard to hear. Even a friends-with-benefits relationship would suffice. I took in a steadying breath as I carefully placed the dishes into the sink to be washed.

"Who said anything about a relationship?" I countered as light-heartedly as I could.

"Right."

"Calvin, I told you day one that we can keep things casual, friendly."

"Yes, you did." Calvin sounded relieved. "I'll wash the dishes."

"It's fine."

"You cooked, I'll clean." Hands on my hips, he shuffled me aside. "Do you have a dress for the gala?"

"Dress? Gala?" I stuttered, the subject taking a 180. "No?"

Calvin laughed. "You're asking me? I don't know what you packed."

"Certainly not a gala-worthy dress."

"Well, I want you to be my plus one for the gala." He said. "It'll be our last night together after all."

I nodded somberly. "It will be."

"So, I want you to take my card and buy a new dress for the event." Calvin held up his hand before I could protest. "Consider it a thank you for everything you've done in my office."

I pursed my lips, not happy. He spent too much on me already, from buying me at that auction. If I'm forced to buy myself a dress, I'll be sure not to spend a fortune, and to use my own card.

"Wow." Kelsie gushed when she got into the Ferrari. "There's a story here."

"A lot has happened this week."

She buckled in. "Tell me when we get to the mall. I want your full attention on the road."

"Hey!" I glanced at her. "Are you implying that I'm a bad driver?"

"I would never say that to the driver behind the wheel of a too-fast car that she's never driven before."

I pressed down lightly on the gas pedal.

"Do you want to get a ticket, Speed Demon?"

With a laugh, I let off the gas. She had a point. It wouldn't look good to get a ticket while in Calvin's car once we're on the highway, though it'll be a different story. I couldn't stop the smile, anticipating the thrill skittering through my veins at the mere thought. In fact, Kelsie started to laugh when I picked up speed on the highway.

I took us to one of the high-end shopping areas in Stramford, not because I have Calvin's card, but because there are good-quality clothes that I can afford. There are still hints of my snooty, rich up-bringing that are so ingrained in me that I can't shake them from my past, such as my love for expensive, high-quality clothing. I know there is an area in the city that's very reminiscent of Rodeo. If I still had my family's money, I'd be able to afford it.

"Okay." Kelsie said after I'd parked the Ferrari. "Something is clear-ly weighing on your mind if we're here."

"You could say that." I mumbled. "I also need a dress for a gala."

"Ooo, fancy. What's the gala for?"

"It's to thank investors and introduce a new product."

"Product?" Kelsie exclaimed. "Since when did Harrington and Sons get into product selling?"

I laughed. "Never. It's for CalTorAtt, I'm a plus one."

"Oh my gosh, I love their games." She squealed. "You are so lucky to get a first look at what's coming. They've been hinting at a new game for nearly two years now. No, that's not quite true. About a year ago, they stated some bugs had been discovered and that there would be a delay. Nothing has been announced since."

The Nicolette issue—I thought—the timeline fits. Kelsie contin-ued gushing over the games CalTorAtt has produced and how much she loves them. I didn't realize the company had so many games. I only have one of them on my phone.

After two stores where I couldn't find a single dress that called to me, Kelsie suggested we break for coffee. I knew her true intention. My time for confessing has come.

"Okay, spill." She ordered.

I let out a long sigh and told her everything. Starting with what Steven found in the company financials, all the way up to my day with Calvin yesterday. Nothing was left out while I tried to keep it short and to the point. Kelsie sat there, her iced coffee melting as she listened intently. When I finished, I finally took a sip of my frozen frappe and waited for her judgment.

"That's a lot." Kelsie finally said. "And it's only been a week."

"Yeah." I admitted, not sure what else to say.

"There's only one part I want to focus on. It's your feelings for Calvin."

My cheeks heated. "What do you mean? I don't have any particular feeling for him, except maybe lust."

"You can lie to yourself, but you can't lie to me. I heard it in your voice when you talked about him." A grin broke out on her face. "You really, really like him."

"No." I scoffed, trying to sound nonchalant. "I don't like him that way. I can't like him that way. It'll never work anyway."

Her grin only seemed to widen. "This dress, for the gala, you're trying to find the perfect one that'll leave him on his knees and speechless."

Am I? It never even crossed my mind. Or maybe it did, and subconsciously, that's what I'm doing. I don't know. The conversation with Calvin this morning put me off kilter. I slouched in the chair, cradling my frozen frappe to my chest as I sipped the concoction through the straw.

"You don't have to worry about the dress, I know exactly what we should look for." Kelsie's grin faded into concern. "I want to know what you meant by 'you can't like him that way'."

I winced. "I didn't say that."

She brought her mouth to the straw of her iced coffee and sipped. Maintaining eye contact, she waited. Best friends really know how to squeeze every bit of information out of the other who has been holding back. If the tables were turned, I could do the same to her. However, I called her out for this shopping trip partly because I needed help finding a dress, but also because I wanted to talk to her about Calvin.

"Calvin had a really bad relationship." I finally said, leaning in to speak in hushed tones. "He doesn't want a new relationship."

"Ah." She said as if everything now made sense. "You're at a cross-roads. Either you respect his wishes and end up with a broken heart. Or you subtly try to convince him to have a relationship with you, and if it doesn't work, you'll still be walking away with a broken heart."

"Or I put up walls now before it's too late." I countered.

Kelsie shook her head. "It's already too late."

I let out a defeated sigh. "He reminded me this morning he's not looking for any relationship, and it hurt to hear it."

"Because you're you, you'll respect his wishes and walk away after the gala." Her lips pursed disapprovingly. "Sometimes I wish you were greedier."

"What is that supposed to mean?"

She patted my hand. "I'll have the ice cream ready."

I narrowed my eyes at her. "I can be greedy."

"Look, I think he's not being honest with himself. He told you about his upbringing, he showed you his childhood home, and he was vulnerable with you. I highly doubt he did all of that to get you into his bed." Kelsie stood, collecting her iced coffee. "Let's go find you that perfect gala dress. You still have a week, make the most of it."

Sixteen

Calvin

MONDAY CAME WAY TOO fast. I wish I could have frozen time, especially on Saturday, when I could have doubled the pleasure of being with Anya. With Anya out to find a dress for the gala, I didn't see her for most of Sunday. It was my fault, really. I should have gone with her. Being near Anya did odd things to my heart. I know getting too tangled with the woman would be dangerous, but I can't resist this allure she has over me.

Having Anya work at the table away from my desk was safer. With her near, combined with her honeysuckle scent, all I crave is to devour her. I'd never get any work done. Plus, the office, as I've learned, is not exactly a wise place to have sex, or even steal a kiss. Gossip runs rampant among employees, and it's impossible to stop it. I don't want to be the center of it—again.

My desk phone rang. "This is Sinclair."

"Mr. Sinclair, this is front desk security." A young-sounding voice said. "There's a Miss Iris Calhoon here. She says she made an appointment, but there's nothing on the expected visitor's log."

"Send her up." I ordered before hanging up. "That makes twice."

"What makes twice?" Anya asked.

"Miss Calhoon." I said without explanation. "She's on her way up."

"Maybe she's coming with good news."

"Doubtful. I'm not sure what I'll do if she couldn't fulfill the gala requirements over the weekend."

"Don't worry, Calvin." Anya came over, massaging my shoulders. "The one trait I took with me from home is the ability to save any event, no matter how last-minute. Mother would have been proud of the connections I've made."

"Calvin." Miss Calhoon knocked on the open door. "I'm here about the gala."

Anya returned to her spot while Miss Calhoon took a seat in front of me. I did not miss the curl of her lip, directed at Anya, as she walked by. It's those kinds of games that were part of the reason I didn't date after Nicolette.

"Miss Calhoon, what news do you have for me?"

She pulled a file folder from her large purse and placed it on my desk. "This is an invoice for all the time my company has put into this gala. We are unable to fulfill your requests and are pulling out."

"The biggest change was the need for a bartender and the catering options."

"Lafoyette could not accommodate, and no one else in our contacts could be ready for this Friday." She said. "I have reached out to friends in this field and told them about our interactions. I thought it only fair to warn you that you won't find anyone to help you for this gala, or any future events."

"I will give this invoice to finance." I said politely, a stiff smile on my lips. "Thank you for your time, Miss Calhoon."

Chin in the air, she briskly walked out of my office. I looked over to Anya for guidance, but she wasn't there. Frowning, I collected the invoice to take to Wyatt and found her out in the hall. I don't know who she was talking to on the phone, and I wasn't sure that I wanted to know. She was twirling her hair around her finger. I've never seen her do that before, but I've seen other women do that when they are flirting. A dark coil of something formed inside me at the sight. I averted my gaze before I did something stupid—like kiss her so she never considers flirting with anyone but me.

"Wyatt, this invoice needs to be paid." I said when I entered his office.

"Don't pay it." Anya rushed in behind me. "I think you may have been conned."

"What are you talking about?" Wyatt looked at her, then at me. "What am I supposed to be paying?"

"An invoice from Miss Calhoon." I said, handing it over.

Wyatt's gaze flickered over to Anya. "You said we're being conned?"

"Let me see the invoice." She held out her hand.

Wyatt handed it over without question. She took a picture of the logo before handing it back. My friend looked to me for answers. All I could do was shrug. I had no idea what she was doing or what she was talking about.

"I've worked with the owner of Lafoyette before. She told me that Iris Calhoon not only claimed to be an employee of CalTorAtt, but she had also cancelled the service on Friday. Turns out, last month Miss Calhoon had booked Lafoyette to serve hors d'oeuvres for the gala, not a full course meal like she had claimed."

"Why would she lie?" I asked, genuinely confused.

Her phone pinged. "She lied because Miss Calhoon's so-called company doesn't exist. My friend just confirmed that it's fake."

"How?"

"She works in marketing and has programs that can pull up any logo created for a legitimate company." She explained. "All companies have to register their logo so it doesn't get copied by an up-and-coming business."

"I'll have my brother look into this." Wyatt proclaimed. "In the meantime, you have to scramble to piece this gala back together."

"Not a problem." Anya turned to leave. "Stay tuned for good news."

After she left, Wyatt let out a sigh. I turned to him, not realizing until that moment that my gaze lingered on Anya. My friend was leaning back in his chair, eyes closed as he does when he's frustrated and counting silently in his head.

"First Nicolette, now this Iris Calhoon." He grumbled. "I think this new game of ours is cursed."

"What else could go wrong?" I asked, forcing it to sound cheerful.

Wyatt opened his eyes to glare at me. "You're going to regret saying that."

"Seriously, Wyatt." I took a seat. "We recovered from Nicolette's betrayal."

"It took us months to recover from her thievery. Hector had to work his team overtime to revamp the code so the game didn't become a duplicate of something HITGames would surely put out."

"With Anya, we can save the gala."

"Bad luck, and curses, always come in threes."

"That's just superstition." I waved him off, despite the unease forming in my gut.

"It's your funeral." He said.

"Why is it Calvin's funeral?" Hector questioned, entering the office.

"He doesn't believe curses come in threes." Wyatt declared, as if something dawned on him. "It might involve the new game, but two women have screwed you over because of it, Calvin."

I glared at him. "Anya is not the third curse."

"I hope not." Hector said. "I love the woman."

I nearly choked on my own saliva. "Love?"

"Yeah, like how I love you guys. She's a perfect fit. I plan on seeing her even after she leaves." He frowned. "By the way, did you set up a meeting with Marcel?"

"No." I frowned at him. "Why?"

"Because I saw him enter your office."

I scrambled out of the chair and headed for my office. What I saw made my blood boil. Anya was facing him, unmoving as Marcel cupped the back of her neck and leaned in close. She wasn't doing anything to stop him. Could Wyatt have been right, and I'm watching the third curse unfold before my eyes?

"Marcel." I said, announcing my presence.

Anya physically jolted. She shoved at Marcel and slapped him across the face. She lifted her leg as if to kick him in the groin, but I came up behind her, placing my hands on her shoulders. I felt Anya ease under my touch, and she lowered her leg.

"Why are you here, Marcel?" I asked, squeezing Anya's shoulders lightly. "I told you CalTorAtt doesn't want to do any business with you."

"Anya." He flashed her a smug smile. "We go way back. I was checking up on her."

I tilted my head down so I could see the side of her face. "You know him?"

"First name only." She gritted her teeth. "It has been years since I've seen this snake."

"So harsh after our night together." Marcel's smile grew, a spark of interest in his brown eyes. "It was quite memorable."

"Are you referring to the night you got me drunk to take advantage of me?" She countered.

Anya went to take a step forward, but I held her back. There was no mistaking the anger and hurt in her tone. I wanted to wrap my arms around her for comfort, but didn't want to give Marcel any more leverage on me. It took quite a lot of restraint on my part not to punch him.

"I'd hardly call our time together anything but fun."

"That's enough, Marcel." I intervened. "What business could possibly bring you here?"

His gaze shifted to me, and the smug attitude was wiped instantly. "I heard that your gala planning isn't going so well, and I thought I'd offer my assistance."

My jaw clenched. "How did you hear that?"

"I have my connections." He shrugged.

"I appreciate the offer, but your assistance is not needed." I told him firmly. "You can remove yourself from the premises of your own volition, or I can contact security."

Marcel scowled his displeasure on his way out. I came around to face Anya. Tears threatened to put out the fire in her eyes. There's a story here, one I hope she'll open up and divulge. I cupped her cheeks, running my thumbs under her eyes and placed my forehead against hers.

"Anya." I said softly.

She took in a deep breath, letting it out shakily. "I'm okay."

"I'm here if you need to talk."

She blinked back the tears, and her lips tilted upward. "I have a gala to fix."

"I can take you home." I insisted.

"No. Marcel was a drunken mistake, a piece of my past that I can't erase." Anya tilted her face up to kiss me. "I'm here with you, that's what matters now."

Seventeen

Anya

I couldn't focus. Marcel showing up here put me on edge. It's true that he got me drunk and took advantage of my inebriated state, but that's not the whole story. I was fully conscious and consenting in the morning. I had kicked him out only after seeing a few cryptic texts from some woman pop up on his phone while he was in the bathroom. Paranoid, I searched my apartment and found signs that my laptop had been tampered with, thanks to the fail-safes Shane had added when I started working for David. Otherwise, I might have never noticed.

Panicked, I looked for other signs of disturbances in my apartment. I had found the drawers of my desk rifled through, and books on my bookshelf that weren't pushed back to their original position. It was all subtle, but I've always had an eye for detail. It was another thing my mother drilled into me.

Marcel was looking for something. Pissed at myself for how I'd gotten into the situation, I had tried looking him up online. I had no last name to help in the search, and I couldn't find a picture of him either. On a whim, I had tried the woman's name that had popped up on his phone. Her, I found, she was a rival of David's, both of them working to win the favour of a large company. I had called Shane about the situation immediately, afraid I might have screwed up David's opportunity.

"Anya." Calvin's voice broke through my memories. "Are you sure you're okay?"

"Yeah." I stood, collecting my phone and purse. "I just need some fresh air."

"On the seventh floor, there's a terrace you can use. We made that floor a serene spot for employees when they need to destress."

I nodded and left. The seventh floor really was a serene spot. Soft music played the moment the elevator doors opened, and the lights on this level were dimmed. I found rooms equipped with massage chairs and another with lounging chairs. There was a room that looked like it was designed for yoga or meditation. What I needed was the outdoors, and as much fresh air as Stramford can offer. I would have much preferred to take Calvin's bike outside the city, but I need to make a few phone calls, so the terrace will have to do.

There were two people on the terrace playing a game of chess. I smiled at them when they looked up, then went to find a spot that wouldn't disturb them. The terrace wrapped around the building, and I found a spot tucked, almost hidden from view, among the plants that were scattered throughout the floor. Settling in, I made my first phone call.

"Anya, are you okay?" David's concerned tone rang clearly through the line when he picked up. "Do you need rescuing?"

I relaxed instantly at his voice and smiled. "I need some information. Can you help?"

"That depends on what you need."

"Why were you going to work for HITGames?"

David let out a sigh, and I could picture him running a hand over his face. "Your brother is in need of legal aid."

"What did he do?" I held up a hand, even though he couldn't see it. "Scratch that, I don't want to know."

"It was your father who came to me with the proposition of being on retainer for the whole company. I've been stalling with having the contract signed, trying to find a way out of it. I've never really liked your brother."

"Then I bulldozed my way through that meeting."

"CalTorAtt already had a meeting with us." I heard the smile in his voice. "I wanted to see their worth."

I chuckled. "You mean you wanted to use them as a 'conflict of interest' client to be able to turn HITGames down."

"Exactly. Why are you asking about all of this?"

I heard the subtle sound of his chair rolling back. He was either leaning back with his legs outstretched or he was getting up to grab a drink from the bar cart in his office. I twisted to look out over the city. Cars honked below, people walked up and down the sidewalk while the sun beat down, reflecting off the tall glass buildings. Despite it being business hours, the streets were still busy.

"Marcel showed up at CalTorAtt." I said. "He said he had a meeting with Calvin, but when Calvin showed up, he was adamant that the company wants nothing to do with Marcel. Then Marcel changed his tune and said he could help with the gala. Only minutes before, Miss Iris Calhoon had backed away from her duties, leaving CalTorAtt's gala preparations stranded."

"I know that name. Iris Calhoon." He mused. "It'll come to me."

"I've already confirmed she's not an event planner and was trying to con this company."

"Did you tell Mr. Sinclair about your past run-in with Marcel?"

"Sort of." I brought my knees up and wrapped my arms around them. "Calvin knows that Marcel got me drunk and took advantage of me."

"Why didn't you tell him everything?" David asked softly.

"I don't know."

"Remember, Anya, you don't owe Mr. Sinclair anything. So don't feel bad about not telling him."

"I know." I agreed. "I'm just embarrassed."

"Your past isn't one full of luxuries. I know you've had dark moments." He continued. "I know you, Anya, my love for you has never diminished."

"David." I said his name on an exasperated sigh.

"I don't want to put you in a cage. I love your spirit, Peregrine, always have."

I remained silent. When it comes to me, I know he's honest. We have a history and a great friendship, but I've grown. I don't love him the way I used to when we were younger. Back then, I thought David Harrington was going to be my whole world, and nothing would be able to tear us apart. Then, I experienced the real world when I went to college. I changed. I discovered what I really wanted in life and for myself. I want Calvin Sincalir. I fell for him hard and fast after that first Sunday when we took time to get to know each other.

"David, can you tell me if you've heard anything about Marcel working for HITGames?" I forced my mind back to my phone call.

"I'll look into it." He said, sounding defeated or maybe only disappointed. Hard to say without seeing his face. "I'm always here for you."

"I know." I hung up, fished a business card from my purse and made my next phone call.

"This is Detective Henley."

"Detective, this is Anya Wright. I'm not sure if you remember me."

"Yes, I remember you, Miss Wright. How can I help you?"

"Did Wyatt ask you to look into a man by the name of Marcel?"

He went silent. "Why do you ask?"

"He's." I hesitated, took a deep breath, then spoke. "I don't know his last name, never have, but I do know he's a fixer."

"Fixer? What kind of fixer? No, how do you even know that?" He shot off rapid-fire questions. "Will this cause trouble for my brother?"

"I was used by him once." I forced the words out.

"Miss Wright, you seem to be full of information."

An odd sound escaped my lips. It wasn't a laugh, but not quite a snort either. "I can't tell if that's a compliment or a criticism."

He sighed heavily. "Unfortunately, I'm not sure myself."

There was a lull in the conversation. I tightened my grip around my knees. Today is not my day. The memory of Marcel made me sick. For what he did to me. For what I let him do to me. I can't bring myself to call it rape, because despite being drunk, I did flirt and I did fully participate the next morning—before I kicked him out.

I hate myself for being deceived and exploited by Marcel. He used me to gather information on Harrington and Sons because of my position with David. I never told David, but Marcel is also part of the reason I asked to be transferred to another department. I didn't want to be used against him ever again.

"Miss Wright?" Detective Henley's voice rang in my ear. "Are you still there?"

"I am." I answered meekly. "Marcel showed up in Calvin's office today, that's the only reason I'm calling you about him. I don't want him to screw over this company, or their employees, just because some outside source is paying him to do so."

"Would you have any idea as to why this fixer showed up today?"

I shook my head, remembered he wouldn't be able to see me over the phone, then answered him verbally. "No. I suspect that the gala will be his last chance to do his job, if he hasn't already."

"I'll look into it." He hesitated. "Are you alright, Miss Wright? You don't sound like yourself."

"Thank you, Detective, I'm fine." I said before hanging up.

I won't be alright until Marcel is out of the picture. It's doubtful that the police can do anything about him. The more I sat in my spot under the sun, the more I stewed, and the worse the situation got in my head. Last week, Calvin said that Marcel took him to the auction. Marcel saw me there. There's no way he didn't notice me on that stage. If he can't complete the job he was paid for, he will certainly blackmail Calvin. Buying a human won't reflect well on him or the company if it gets out. Kelsie was right. I'm going to wind up with heartbreak.

"Anya."

I startled. Calvin stood nearby, not close enough for his shadow to signal his presence, and I didn't hear him either. I sat up straight and wiped under my eyes at unshed tears. Calvin took the final strides to be at my side. He settled beside me, coaxed my legs across his lap, and scooted closer.

"You can cry if you want." He cupped my cheek. "It's okay."

That was it. Permission was given. Tears flowed freely. Calvin drew me closer. I gripped his dress shirt and let out all my emotions. The pain, the hatred, the fear, every negative emotion I've kept bottled up since that one night with Marcel came rushing out of me in this moment. It was not pretty. Calvin didn't say anything, only held me tight, rubbing up and down my back soothingly. I needed this more than I ever imagined. In this moment, I didn't have to be strong anymore because Calvin became my strength.

Eighteen

Calvin

THIS WEEK HAS BEEN a whirlwind of events. It started with Miss Calhoon's failure to prepare for the gala and her trying to con the company out of a hefty sum of money, then Marcel's unexpected visit and his past connection to Anya. Wyatt's brother had raided the underground auction this week, too. No one was there for an arrest, but he did find all the contracts stored in cabinets.

Cameron and his team reviewed every contract and questioned all the buyers. He didn't find the contract I signed when I bought Anya. I didn't tell her because I didn't want her to worry, but it didn't stop me from worrying. I want to burn the contract, destroy any evidence that could harm Anya or CalTorAtt.

I spent every night with Anya in my bed. It was the only time I could relax. Finally, it was the night of the gala—my last night with Anya.

I waited in the kitchen for Anya to finish getting ready. My stomach was doing flip-flops, concerned over how the investors would perceive the gala. I had no doubt that Anya wouldn't have been able to piece it all together in a couple of days. My nerves also stemmed from not wanting this to be my last night with Anya. I want her to stay, but does she want to stay?

"Okay." Anya's voice drifted down the stairs. "I'm ready."

I looked up and my breath caught. Anya is a beautiful woman, but tonight she's even more stunning. Her raven hair was set in waves over one shoulder, and the makeup was simple, accentuating her features and making the green in her hazel eyes pop. The dress. God, the dress. The purple fabric hugged her curves as if it were sewn to her body, flaring gently from her hips to the floor. My mind filled with images of fucking her in that dress, the fabric shielding our connected bodies from view, and my mouth on hers to swallow every sound she would make.

"Do you like it?" She asked, spinning quickly so the skirt flared slightly.

I couldn't find the words and could only nod while I reached down to adjust myself. The smile she shot me kick-started my heart, and my knees nearly buckled. Anya turned to head to the garage, giving me her back. I had caught glimpses of ink during our time together, but the backless dress seemed to frame the entire piece of art. I reached out, placing my hands on her hips to stop her and just stared at the master piece.

Anya looked over her shoulder at me. "It's a Peregrine Falcon, the fastest animal on the planet."

I traced a finger gently along a wing. "It looks like it'll fly right off your shoulder."

"I got it while I was in college. A symbol of my love of speed."

"It must have cost a fortune to have your whole back tattooed."

"My father provided me a small allowance while I was in school, before he cut me off." She explained. "I had saved a portion and used that for the tattoo."

I kissed the head of the bird near her shoulder. "It's stunning."

"Thank you."

"We should go before I decide staying home would be much more fun."

Anya laughed, stepping away from me. We took the Ferrari to The Sunset Palace. We had arrived early, so I could greet the investors as they entered. The small event room didn't look so small anymore. Anya's simple decorating created a subtle yet rich atmosphere. The walls were covered in tulle, with little lights sparkling behind the fabric. Tall cocktail tables were scattered around the room, each with a tight white tablecloth and a small arrangement in the center. A bartender was set up against a wall for the night.

I couldn't believe she pulled this gala together in only a few days. She had left my side to chat with the wait staff, the chef, and the bartender. Despite the simplicity, I still felt uncomfortable in this luxurious space. Before I knew it, Anya had shuffled me to the entrance, and I began greeting the investors.

Thankfully, she stayed by my side, which helped to ease the tension in my shoulders. After about fifteen minutes, Anya instructed me to mingle. People were still slowly trickling in. I surveyed the room, a frown forming. I didn't recognize many of the attendees, since there were non-investors in this room.

"Anya." I whispered into her ear when she slid next to me with a drink. "There are more than I invited here."

"Events like this draw out more people than you invite." She looked around the room. "I recognize one or two from the media. That could be good for the company."

"Media? How did they find out about this?" Panic made my voice rise.

Anya put a hand on my arm. "The media have connections everywhere. One of your investors could have let slip about the gala."

"Then how did they get in?"

"The doors were open, and you didn't restrict this to an invitation-only event." She studied my face. "Do you want them escorted out?"

Slowly, I shook my head. "That would look bad for the company."

She studied my face a little longer, patted my arm, then walked away. I watched her blend into the crowd. I felt lonely without her next to me. A waiter walked by with some sort of hors d'oeuvre that I snagged off the tray and popped into my mouth. I don't know what I ate, but it was delicious, and it gave me something to do aside from following her when I have investors to talk to.

"Well done." Hector came up from behind me and slapped me on the back just as I swallowed the bit of food. "This is a good turnout."

"If it weren't for Anya, none of this would have happened." I answered after a small coughing fit. Turning to see both of my business partners. "What are you guys doing here?"

"Anya highly suggested we show up." Wyatt answered, his eyes darting around the room. "We don't have this many investors, do we?"

"No, we don't."

"This should be good for us." Hector said. "I can't wait to reveal the new game."

"We still have time before then." I looked at my watch. "Enjoy the gala until then."

I looked around the room again. Everyone seemed to be enjoying themselves, except no one was using the available space for dancing. I wondered if I should find Anya and ask her to dance as a way to invite others. Just as the thought crossed my mind, I saw her. She was already being pulled to the dancefloor by Mr. Harrington. He spun her before placing a hand on her back to hold her to him as they swayed to the soft music.

Anya was smiling, looking perfectly comfortable in his arms. My stomach dropped. It makes sense she'd be comfortable with him. She's known him for a long time, so I shouldn't feel jealous or disappointed. Hell, they were technically engaged once upon a time. A few other guests joined on the dancefloor, and cameras flashed in my periphery, reminding me that media personnel were present. I, though, couldn't take my eyes off Anya. I wanted to march over and pull her into my arms, but I couldn't get my feet to move. Does she still have feelings for him? Because I can see Mr. Harrington's feelings clearly written on his face.

Nineteen

Anya

DAVID PULLED ME ONTO the dancefloor. I let him, knowing it was the best way to invite others to dance without actually asking them. The music remained soft, almost romantic. I verified there were no upbeat songs on the playlist, as it'll ruin the gala's atmosphere.

"This is a well-organized gala, Anya." David complimented.

"Calvin's vision really came through." I acknowledged.

"With your help." He grinned at me. "I can see your handiwork in the details."

I smiled at him. "Thank you."

David's hand was firm on my back, holding me to him as we swayed gently. It was the sudden tightening of his other hand around mine, and the feel of his shoulders stiffening, that hinted that something was wrong. His smile remained in place, though it wasn't as relaxed as it was a moment ago. The subtle shift wouldn't be noticeable to anyone who doesn't know him as well as I do. His whole life, he's been in the media's spotlight and knows how to mask his true emotions in front of a crowd.

"What's wrong?" I asked softly.

"The enemy has invaded."

My brows furrowed, but he swayed us in a way so I could see the crowd without it being suspicious. Marcel, my brother, and his fiancée were out there among the guests. I scanned for Calvin. He hadn't noticed them. In fact, his eyes were glued to me. I forced myself to maintain the smile, not wanting to alert him of any trouble. Those three are definitely trouble.

"You need to get them out of here." I told David. "I'll keep Calvin occupied. Have Hector and Wyatt help you. Actually, I think Wyatt's brother, Detective Henley, is around here somewhere."

David looked down at me with a puzzling expression I couldn't read.

"Please, David." I begged. "This is a big night for Calvin and the company. I don't want anything to shake his confidence."

He kissed my cheek. "Because I love you."

He stepped away from me, and I went to Calvin. "Dance with me?"

Calvin's gaze shifted to David's retreat. I couldn't have him spotting the party crashers. Taking his hand, I tugged him to the dancefloor. Calvin refocused on me. I wrapped my arms around his neck, and his arms encircled my waist. My body relaxed instantly at his touch.

"The gala is going really well." I told him.

"You did an amazing job pulling it together." He shifted our position, holding one of my hands and his other on my back, just as David had. "You really are amazing, Anya."

"This is all your vision." I pressed in closer. "The investors I spoke to are genuinely pleased to have been a part of CalTorAtt and its journey."

Calvin's lips thinned. "When this gala is over, there's something I want to talk to you about."

"Okay?" I asked curiously. "Can I have a hint as to the topic?"

Calvin stopped our swaying and stared into my eyes as if searching for an answer. Then the hand on my back skittered up my spine to the base of my skull, and he kissed me. I leaned into him, my eyes closing, and my mouth opening to him. Kissing Calvin settled something deep inside, something that I can't quite name but know I need.

He pulled back, running his thumb just under my bottom lip. "Later, I promise."

"Tease." I barely managed to say. It came out too breathy.

Calvin grinned triumphantly. "Work first, then play."

He pulled me off the floor. I clung to his arm, feeling unsteady in my heels. If that kiss was a hint at what he wanted to talk to me about, then my hope is that he'll want to pursue a relationship after tonight. A real one, not one created through a contract.

As much as I want to hold onto that hope, I know it can't last. Not after tonight. Not after he learns about my connection to HITGames. Calvin will feel betrayed. I didn't want to hurt him, and if my brother never showed his face at this gala, the guillotine hovering above me would feel so ominous.

Calvin stopped in front of his business partners. "I think it's time."

Hector put a hand to his chest, trying desperately not to grin. "Anya, how dare you? I thought we'd be together forever."

I rolled my eyes, thankful he knows how to lighten the mood—even if he doesn't realize it. The smile he had been holding back bloomed on his face. With his friend's comment, Calvin had tugged me subtly closer. Wyatt still eyed me suspiciously. I could feel that guillotine dropping an inch for every second he stared. I get it. He doesn't want me to hurt his friend the way Nicolette had. Unintentionally, it's exactly what I'm going to do.

"I think now's a good time for your announcement." I repeated Calvin's earlier comment. "Before it gets too late in the evening."

I went with them to the platform, which was large enough for them to stand on without it interfering too far into the room. This gave them some height over the crowd. I picked up a microphone and addressed the crowd to gain their attention. I thanked everyone for coming, then introduced the founders and CEOs of CalTorAtt before passing the mic over.

Stepping down, I joined the crowd eager to watch the presentation. Unfortunately, David came up to whisper in my ear that my brother is demanding to see me. It's the last thing I wanted to do, but there has to be an ulterior motive behind the demand. So I went. David led me out of the gala to a room marked as an admin office, behind the front desk. Detective Henley stood by the door, watching my brother pace the length of the room.

"Jensen." I said coolly. "You wanted to see me?"

"Anya, my dear sister." He said far too sweetly. "I'm so happy to see you."

Jensen opened his arms wide as if to hug me, but both David and the detective blocked him. I had stepped back, too, not wanting to be touched by him. He looked so much thinner and paler than the last time I'd seen him. Granted, it had been over ten years.

"We may be related by blood, but you are not my brother." I declared, resolute in my words. "I have not been a part of the family in years, and I never will be ever again."

"That's harsh, little sister."

"Why are you even here, Jensen?"

"I had to see what the competition had going on." He plopped himself down in a chair with a sly grin. "I see you're being well treated."

I crossed my arms and narrowed my eyes. "What exactly do you mean by that?"

"Calvin Sinclair must have been truly heartbroken after Nicolette if he had to buy your attention and affection."

"Calvin didn't buy my attention."

"Oh really?" He looked like the cat that caught the canary. "That's not what the contract implies. By the way, where is the emerald necklace?"

A twitch in Detective Henley's hand was the only indication that my brother's words got to him. I don't understand why, though. He had all the contracts from the underground auction. Either Jensen has a mole in the force, or he's connected to the underground auction somehow. David had shifted slightly to eye me. Me? I've mastered the technique of not reacting to anything my brother says.

When I didn't react the way he wanted me to, Jensen clicked his tongue and slouched in the chair. "I really don't understand why Father favours you."

"Favours me?" I scoffed. "He disinherited me."

"He allowed you to go to college. He allowed you to be free. He made you CEO of HITGames." His voice and posture rose with each point.

"He did what?"

I looked to David. His furrowed brows matched my confusion. At least I wasn't the only one who didn't know that little fact.

Jensen laughed bitterly. "If your fiancée had accepted our father's offer, he would have learned the truth. All these years, I've only been the acting CEO. Father truly believes that you'll come back to the family, and when you do, he'll lavish you with everything he's been holding onto. I'm no heir to the Wright name. You are."

I couldn't process all of that. It didn't make sense. Was he lying to me? But then, why would he do that? I took a moment to look around the room for the first time. Jensen was the only one here. Dread crept up my spine.

"Where is Marcel?" I touched Detective Henley's arm.

"He was escorted off the premises by hotel security." The detective explained.

"What about Nicolette? The woman with Jensen?"

"There was no woman." He frowned at me. "Nicolette, is she the same as-?"

"Unfortunately." I grumbled, cutting him off.

With no time to waste, I turned and left the office. She must still be at the gala. If Calvin spots her, his entire night will be crushed by the insecurities that she created.

Twenty

Calvin

"Thank you, everyone." I said into the microphone when Anya handed it over. "Thank you for coming to tonight's gala. Thank you, Anya, for helping to put it all together." There was polite clapping. "This night was created so that we at CalTorAtt could show our appreciation to all of you who have invested in our company over the years."

I handed the microphone over to Wyatt and stepped back. My eyes found Anya in the crowd, her focus on me until Mr. Harrington came up behind her. He whispered something in her ear, and then they left together in a rush. Something was wrong. I wanted to follow, but Hector's hand on my arm halted me. I looked over at him, and he shook his head subtly. Hands in fists, I held my ground. He's right, I need to stay and represent CalTorAtt.

"We couldn't have made it this far without all of you." Wyatt was saying. "So, in addition to our appreciation, we also wanted to make an advanced announcement."

Hector accepted the microphone next and clicked a button on the device in his hand. Behind him, the logo of our newest game appeared.

It took us a year to get to this point after Nicolette. The low rumble of murmurs made me nervous. I couldn't tell if this announcement and launch would be well-received or not.

"We have a new game." Hector beamed. "Crystal Realm. This is more than a match-three game. This is also an adventure game."

He clicked through slides showcasing screenshots of the game and explaining how to play. Hector's excited tone heightened the intrigue among the crowd. At midnight, this game will launch on all platforms. We'll have to wait and see how well the public takes it. They are what matters most. They are the gamers, our customers.

With the announcement done, I slipped down into the crowd to search for Anya. There had to be a good reason why she left. I wanted to know her opinion on the new game. Among the congratulatory slaps and handshakes of investors, a flash of blonde hair in a red dress caught my eye. It wasn't Anya, but I really hoped I was seeing things.

I followed the woman in red. When she turned around, I regretted my decision. Fresh pain invaded my system as if this woman's betrayal had happened yesterday. The gala around me blurred, and all I saw was her.

"Nicolette." My voice sounded strained to my ears, and there was nothing I could do about it. "What are you doing here?"

"Congratulations on the new game." She batted her eyes and clapped her hands together like she was going to clap. "I'm so proud of you."

No thanks to you. I wanted to say it, but the words stuck in my throat. Nicolette closed the gap between us. She trailed a perfectly manicured finger along my cheek, then down to my chest, where she flattened her palm and stayed. I couldn't move. Frozen to the spot with pain and hatred and the tiniest bit of hope. That hope made me angry. My hands clenched as I inwardly fought my ragged emotions.

"You shouldn't be here." I ground out.

"But I missed you." She purred. "We had such a good time together. Don't you remember?"

Vividly, though I wish I didn't. Out of nowhere, Nicolette's hand was pulled away from my person. Anya stood there with my ex's wrist in her hand. Relief flooded me at the sight of her. I wanted to reach out and wrap her in my arms, show Nicolette that I've moved on, but there was something in Anya's expression that kept me immobile. There was a fury in her glare that didn't make sense to me.

"Tsk, tsk." Anya said, her voice laced with hatred yet level in tone. "You shouldn't be touching another man, Nicolette, not with your fiancée nearby."

"Anya Wright, it's been too long." Nicolette yanked her wrist back. "We should really take time to catch up."

"You and I were never friends."

"Maybe not, but we will be family soon."

Family? I looked to Anya, a look of disgust flashing across her face before she could catch herself. I didn't understand what was going on. The words spoken between the two women were simple, but the context was complicated. Anya stepped between Nicolette and me, then leaned back into me as if I could give her strength.

"You may be marrying into the Wright name, but you'll always be a Raines."

Nicolette's face contorted into anger. A look I've never seen on her before. It was quite interesting. So many questions floated around in my mind. One thing stuck out to me that I needed clarification on.

"Raines?" I echoed. She had used a different last name when she worked with me. "You used your father's invitation to gain entry, didn't you?"

"Guilty." Nicolette smirked. "It has been such an entertaining night."

"What do you mean by that?" A sinking feeling formed in my gut.

"Have a good night's sleep." Nicolette gave a finger wave before sashaying away.

Anya turned to face me, concern in her eyes. She cupped my cheek. "You're not looking too good. Should we head out ourselves?"

I wrapped my fingers around hers. "How do you know Nicolette? What did she mean by you'll be family soon?"

Anya's lips thinned. "I think we need to go somewhere a little quieter for that particular conversation."

I didn't like the implication of those words. Maybe Wyatt was right, women are my curse. I didn't want to believe it. I didn't want Anya to be the third in my recent line of bad relationships with women. Taking my hand, Anya led me out of the gala.

"Where are you taking me, Anya?"

"I'm not sure." She admitted.

I tugged her to a stop before we made it to the stairs. Instinct was yelling at me that whatever she has to say will end everything. So, I kissed her, hoping this won't be the last time. I want one more night with her before reality seeps into our little bubble.

"Let's go home." I said.

Anya nodded, letting me lead her out to the Ferrari. Hector and Wyatt can handle closing the gala. I needed to postpone whatever Anya wanted to say in private. I like what we have and want to keep it until the bitter end. Tonight, I won't just fuck Anya, I will make love to her.

Twenty-One

Anya

I SHOULDN'T HAVE INDULGED in the pleasure that is Calvin Sinclair last night because it felt more than just sex, which made me feel even worse. I should have told him about Jensen and HITGames before his lips found mine and we tumbled into bed. Before he woke up, I packed my suitcase, ready to go home and fighting back tears. Our contract is done. I read the articles from last night's gala while I waited for him to wake up.

Calvin finally came downstairs, looked at my suitcase, then at me. "You're packed."

"Contract is over." I stated. "I think we should walk away on a high note."

"What are you talking about?" Calvin ran his hands up and down my arms. "I want you to stay, Anya. I lo-."

I put a finger to his lips, cutting off his words. Tears clogged my throat. I shouldn't have waited for him to wake up for me to say goodbye. I should have left while he still slept because I could feel my heart shattering. Calvin will read those articles. When he does, he will look at me with horror, and then he will say something cruel in the heat of the moment. I didn't want to bear witness to any of it, but I couldn't bring myself to leave without a final goodbye.

"Just remember that I never lied to you." I kissed his cheek and went to the door. "Goodbye, Calvin."

He stared after me, dumbstruck. I could see the confusion and hurt in his eyes. Green eyes that'll haunt my dreams. David was outside waiting for me. Without a word, he took my suitcase and put it in the trunk before sliding behind the wheel of his Cadillac. I took one final look at Calvin, who stood in his doorway, watching the sedan drive away.

"Did you tell him?" David asked after a few blocks of silence.

"No." I said, still fighting the threatening tears.

"You should have. Those articles were full of lies and assumptions."

"I know, but there was also some truth, too."

I may never have Calvin, but he will forever have my heart. I wasn't looking for love, but in the short time together, I fell in love with Calvin Sinclair. David reached over the console and squeezed my hand. That simple gesture broke the dams.

I spent the weekend sulking. Kelsie came over with ice cream, comedy movies, and an ear to listen. She took a moment to read the articles posted, then vented about them on my behalf. It helped a little.

When Monday came, I didn't feel like going into work, but I couldn't stay cooped up forever. My broken heart was still bleeding, but thanks to Kelsie, I was able to mend my shields with duct tape.

Strong enough to counter the looks or comments that were sure to come my way after the articles.

I sat at my desk and worked with a single-mindedness. June fended off any co-workers who looked like they might cause me trouble. She fetched my lunch and ate with me at my desk. She didn't ask me about my supposed vacation or about the articles. The only thing June did was hug me and tell me she was glad I was back.

It'll take time, but I will heal. With Kelsie, June, Shane, and David checking in on me, they helped to keep my head above the proverbial water. What I need to do is stay busy. It's the quiet moments that have my mind wandering to Calvin. He hasn't reached out, and I doubt he ever will.

"Anya, David wants you in his office." Shane came down to fetch me.

"What for?" I asked, not wanting to go.

"Don't argue." He reached for my hand and pulled me up from my chair.

I trailed behind Shane to the elevators. He hit the button for David's executive floor. Walking into his luxurious office, David immediately handed me a glass of something amber. I don't know if it's a scotch or a whisky. It didn't matter. It was strong and burned as it went down.

"Sit." David ordered.

I obeyed and sat at the six-person long table in his office. David and Shane took seats across from me. Clearly, this wasn't a comfort session. This was business.

"I talked to your father." David started up.

"Why did you do that?" I sat up straighter, panicked.

"I needed to confirm what Jensen had said about you being the true heir to the company." David explained calmly. "Sorry it took some time."

"And?"

"It's all true."

Shane went over to David's desk and brought back a file. David opened it and slid papers over, along with a pen. I stared at the black text, not really seeing the words.

"If you sign these, it'll remove your name from HITGames." He explained. "All leadership roles will officially be handed over to Jensen."

I didn't hesitate. I signed the papers. "I want nothing to do with that company, and nothing to do with the Wright family."

"I know." He collected the papers. "Is there anything else I can do?"

I shook my head.

"I can talk to Mr. Sinclair." Shane offered.

Again, I shook my head. "That won't do anything. Those damned articles ruined whatever was growing between us."

"I'm sorry, Anya."

"Me too." I stood. "It's too late now, and nothing can be done to fix the damage those reporters caused."

Twenty-Two

Calvin

I WAS TORTURING MYSELF by re-reading those damned articles. Headlines like *'Lover's Triangle Between Three CEOs'* and *'Merger Between CalTorAtt and HITGames'* had me feeling sick. The articles themselves made the headlines seem mild. Each one was worse than the previous one I had read.

Anya played me like a fool. I should have put the pieces together sooner. Her last name and being disinherited both suggested she had wealth. I could have looked her up, like she had looked me up. I could have confronted her about all of this. I didn't.

Twice now, HITGames have weaselled a woman into my life. Frustrated, I shoved everything off my desk with a roar. I'm such an idiot. Falling in love with Anya Wright was the dumbest thing I've ever done. I should have learned my lesson after Nicolette. I should have steeled my resolve and kept Anya at arm's length.

"Okay, clearly leaving you alone was not a good idea." Hector said, turning his head in the hall. "Wyatt, get in here."

It didn't take long for Wyatt to enter my office. My two friends closed the door, surveyed the mess on the floor, and then looked at each other. The two of them exchanged a look. I watched Hector come around my desk, while Wyatt stayed on the other side.

Hector put his hands on my shoulders, forcing me down. "Sit down."

"I'm cursed to be betrayed by every woman that comes into my life." I griped. "Never again."

"Anya didn't betray you."

"She's the heir to HITGames, and she's still engaged to David Harrington." I waved vaguely to the computer. "The articles explained everything."

"No, they didn't." Wyatt slapped a file on my desk. "This is the background check Cam did on Anya."

I eyed the file like it would bite. "What difference would it make?"

"Before Cam handed it over, he told me two things. First, everyone has a past. Some people learn and grow from it, while others try to hide their past and reinvent themselves."

My friend fell silent. Watching me expectantly. I didn't know what he wanted from me. When I didn't say anything, he rolled his eyes and continued.

"The second thing is that Anya didn't lie. Everything she told him checked out." He pointed at me. "Including what she told him about Marcel."

Did she tell him what Marcel did to her and didn't tell me? Why did she have so many damned secrets? I feel like I knew nothing about Anya Wright.

"I've read the file." Hector squeezed my shoulders. "You should too."

"It won't change anything." I pushed the file away.

Hector reached over me to pull it closer. "You're letting Nicolette rule over your life."

Anger catapulted me to my feet. I turned, grabbing Hector by his shirt and slammed him against the window behind my desk. He held his hands up, palms out.

"Nicolette has nothing to do with this." I growled.

"The betrayal she landed did a number on you." He said far too calmly. "You've layered it over your time with Anya and have convinced yourself they are the same."

"I'm not layering shit."

"Then what exactly is your issue?" Wyatt asked, annoyance in his tone.

I love her. I let her walk away. I'm insecure. I screwed up. My jaw clenched as I tried to work through how best to answer that question.

"She betrayed me." I finally answered.

"How?"

I opened my mouth to answer, but drew a blank. Unlike Nicolette, I couldn't pinpoint how Anya betrayed me.

"Okay." Wyatt said as if agreeing with me. "What else has you so pissed?"

"Anya lied to me." I looked over my shoulder at him.

"When?"

"The articles. She told me she wasn't engaged. She told me she was disinherited. She told me-." I cut myself off, loosening my grip on Hector.

"What else?" Wyatt prodded.

I swallowed hard. "The last thing Anya said to me was to remember that she never lied to me."

Hector let out a low whistle. "Bold woman. You could have taken those words as her last lie, or the last truth you'll ever hear."

"I have a suspicion Anya's been heartbroken these past couple of weeks while you sat here all pissed." Wyatt said.

Heartbroken? The word echoed around my skull. Why would she have been heartbroken? Why do my friends care more about her than they do about me? I held firm to my anger.

"How can the two of you be so calm about all of this?" I bellowed, running my hands through my hair and tugging on the ends. "Three times now this company has been fooled by a woman."

"Only once." Hector said, joining Wyatt on the safer side of the desk.

"Nearly twice." Wyatt added. "If Anya hadn't caught Miss Calhoon's con, then it would have been twice."

"Anya also helped with the gala. Without her, we might not have had one."

"Stop it." I whispered, gripping the back of my chair, then louder. "Stop it! Nothing you say will change what these reporters wrote. Anya didn't tell me anything about HITGames."

Wyatt opened the file he'd brought. "Read the file Cam put together. Your anger toward Anya is misdirected."

I stared at the simple white sheet of paper with black font printed across it. Words, that's all it is. It won't hurt to read what the detective found. Slowly, I sat down and began to read.

I spent hours reading everything Detective Henley amassed. Everything from the background check to all of the articles from Anya's earlier life. The media was all over Anya and her family. Every single thing they did was recorded. She was the crowning jewel—a princess—in high society.

I was such an idiot. I let my insecurities about women, no thanks to Nicolette, ruin whatever was growing between Anya and me.

Everything she'd told me coincides with Cam's research and notes. All truth. Except she never told me about her connection to our biggest competition.

Wyatt's acute assessment of my anger irritated me. I was angry with Anya for walking away without giving me a chance to process the articles after the gala. Then, as the words of the articles sank in, my subconscious knew they were lies, but I couldn't admit it out loud. My anger then turned inward.

I should have never let Anya walk out of my house that horrible Saturday. Out of my grasp and right into David Harrington's car.

I need to get Anya back into my life. I need to apologize. Picking up my phone, I started to make phone calls. There was a lot of work to get done.

Twenty-Three

Anya

THESE PAST TWO WEEKS have been tough mentally and emotionally. Work has been slow, so my mind and heart have often wandered to Calvin. When clients come in to see Bill about the proceedings in their divorce case, I've been wondering whether they've ever felt the heartbreak I've been feeling. Or are anger and misunderstandings guiding these couples toward divorce?

I've been heartbroken before, well, sort of. When David left for university, the ache I felt wasn't quite as strong as it is now. The only difference from then to now is that my mother kept me so busy I didn't have time to miss him, except, of course, at the end of the day when I lay in my bed alone.

Even back then, it took time to ease that ache to a dull numbness until it no longer existed. The same thing will happen again, I'm sure of it. It just might take longer.

When I arrived at work today, there was a crowd around my desk. June and a few other women who work on this floor had all gathered. I could hear the giggles and excited tone to their whispers. What could possibly be so captivating? I tried to peer around them, but I couldn't see past their bodies to whatever had their undivided attention.

"Excuse me." I said with a touch of irritation in my tone, crossed my arms and waited for them to part. "I'd like to get to my desk and start working."

As if one collective, the five, no six, women spun—a mixture of reactions on their faces ranging from a broad grin to a sheepish one. June was the first to separate from the group and return to her desk. The couple with the sheepish grin hurriedly left my desk, leaving three still standing there. With the crowd cleared, I could now see the large floral arrangement sitting on my desk.

"So?" One of them, a blonde, asked. "Who do you think bought these?"

I don't know these three women too well. They have only been working with Harrington and Sons for a month, maybe two. Our paths never really crossed. Since these three all started around the same time, they became quick friends. June befriended them because of their similar ages. It would explain their presence here when they work on the other end of the floor.

"I'll have to read the card." I said matter-of-factly. "These things always come with a card."

"We looked, there's nothing." The redhead smirked. "That tells me that you know this guy."

"How does any of my life matter to you?"

"We're just trying to be friendly, Anya." She scowled. "You're such a cold bitch."

I sat down with a heavy sigh and gently brushed my fingers along the soft petals of a peony. "I like my privacy."

The three girls huffed and marched off. I moved the arrangement from the center of my desk to the side. The purples of the peonies in the arrangement reminded me of the dress I wore at the gala. With the dark green greenery and little white and pink daisies, it was stunning but made my heart ache. My eyes scanned the arrangement for a card, and sure enough, there was none. Doesn't matter who sent them. I'm sure they were meant to brighten my day, so the gesture was nice, but I couldn't bear to look at the flowers.

Some time around noon, a courier stepped off the elevator. He came straight to me since I was the only one here. I had let June have lunch first since I wasn't too hungry right now. My eyes drifted to the courier's arms and the long white box he carried.

"Hi." He said, then looked down at his clipboard. "I'm looking for an Anya Wright."

"That's me." I stood, reaching for the clipboard he handed over. "Who sent it?"

"No idea." He shrugged. "I'm just tasked with delivery."

I took the box and looked down. The long white box had a window on the top, revealing a single red rose. Sitting down with a frown, I opened the box, hoping to find a note this time. I lifted the single stem, bringing the bloom to my nose and breathed in the delicate scent. Twice today, I've received flowers. I picked up the note that was under the flower and read the single word: Peregrine.

With the rose in my hand, I went up to David's office. His secretary wasn't at her desk, probably out for lunch herself. It wouldn't have mattered through. As long as David's not in a meeting, I walk straight into his office. My oldest friend, ex-fiancée, and boss sat in his office chair, watching the door as if he were waiting for me.

"David, what is this?" I held up the flower in question.

"It's a rose, my sweet Peregrine."

"Not what I meant, and you know it."

David laughed. "It was a lure."

I frowned, placing the stem on his desk. "Lure?"

He stood from his desk, coming around and placing his hands on my shoulders. "I think you made a mistake, leaving Calvin the way you did."

My cheeks flushed, and I looked down at our feet. "I had to. If I'd stayed, he would have hated me after reading those articles, and I couldn't bear the thought of seeing that metamorphosis."

"Did you ever consider that leaving would have made it worse?" David lifted my chin. "Without you to differentiate the truth from the lies, he would have no choice but to assume the articles were the truth, and your leaving would have confirmed that."

My gut tightened. I hadn't thought of that. Maybe I should have realized that's what had happened when I hadn't heard from Calvin in two weeks. Though I didn't really give him the impression that I wanted to be with him beyond the contract's time frame.

"Lucky for you, you have me." David smiled. "I let you wallow in your misery, hoping you'd realize your mistake and go to him."

I swallowed hard, staring wide-eyed at him. I couldn't possibly go to Calvin now. What would I say? Would he even want to see me?

"I know you, Anya." He cupped my face. "I also won't let you continue to sulk."

David leaned in and kissed me. I blinked, registering his lips against mine. I stepped back and shoved him away all at once. Once, long ago, David's kiss had curled my toes. Even after our time apart, his kisses were soothing with a hint of need on his part, though he never pushed it. Now they don't do anything for me. I don't want to kiss anyone other than Calvin.

That jolt of realization had me staring at David. Except, he wasn't looking at me. I followed his gaze to the door. Calvin stood there, his hand primed to knock on the frame but frozen in mid-action. Joy and fear fought for dominance within.

"Calvin." I said his name on a sharp intake of breath.

That drew his focus to me, and he gave me a shy smile. "Hi."

David straightened, walked to Calvin and placed a hand on his shoulder. He leaned in and whispered something in Calvin's ear. I don't know what he said, but it hardened Calvin's gaze with determination, and he nodded. David left us. Calvin came into the office, closed the door behind him, and marched closer.

"What are you doing here?" I questioned.

He hesitated in his next step. "I came to see you."

"Why?"

"Because I was an idiot."

My mind couldn't process what was going on. I didn't understand. Calvin watched me. The bold confidence he had started with slipped away, revealing his uncertainty. He shifted on his feet and rubbed the back of his neck.

"Um, did you like the flowers?"

"Flowers?" I repeated.

"Yeah. I was told that purple peonies can represent admiration, respect, and romance." He blushed. "The colour also reminded me of you."

"Oh." My eyes widened. "There was no card. I didn't know."

Calvin frowned. "I put one there."

Someone had to have taken it. Why or who? I had no idea. Right now, I don't care.

"I shouldn't have let you walk out on me that Saturday." Calvin declared. "I was a fool for letting the articles about you and Mr. Harrington and HITGames eclipse our time together."

My heart tightened. Either I was hearing an apology or a confession. I couldn't tell. I held my breath, almost chanting my wish that it would be a confession.

"I let my insecurities, the ones formed by Nicolette, take precedence over everything else." His green eyes stared at me, pleading with me. "I never thought I could fall for another woman, then you came into my life and crashed through every barrier I had constructed with ease."

"What-." My voice clogged with emotion, and I had to clear it before getting any more words out. "What are you trying to say?"

Calvin closed the gap between us, taking my hands in his. "I love you, Anya. If you'll accept me back into your life, I'll take whatever spot you deem fit."

Too many emotions coursed through my body. Elation winning top spot. My heart wanted to burst with joy, my knees wanted to give out in relief, and I swear I felt a prickling of tears in my eyes. Calvin reached up to cup my face, his thumb brushing under my eye with a frown.

"What's wrong?" Concern in his tone.

I wrapped an arm around his neck and kissed him. Nothing was wrong. His confession of love glued my broken heart back together and was a balm to ease the pain. Neither one of us expected to find love in our unusual meeting, but we did. Calvin smiled into the kiss and deepened it.

I pulled back first. "I love you too, Calvin."

He rested his forehead on mine. "Move back in with me."

Pulling his hands away from my face, I took a small step back. "No."

Panic flared up in his dark green eyes. "But I thought-."

"That we'd say that we love each other, then go back to how it was before?"

Embarrassment flushed his cheeks. "Well, um, yes?"

"Calvin, more than anything, I want to be back in your arms, but I think we need to take a step back." I cupped his cheek. "What I mean to say is, we rushed things. We were on a two-week timeline, lust and desire fueled our motives. I want us to start at the beginning, form the base of a relationship, and grow the love we have into something unshakable."

Calvin turned his head to kiss my palm. "Tonight, I'm taking you on a first date. I'll pick you up at six."

I laughed. "You don't even know where I live."

"Then you'll have to give it to me." He pulled out his phone. "Dress elegantly tonight."

My heart fluttered as I gave him my home address. He already has my number from our time together. With one last kiss and a 'see you tonight', Calvin left me in David's office. As one man exited, the other entered.

"So?" David prodded. "Are you two back together?"

"He's taking me on a date." I said with a giggle.

"Good." He kissed the back of my hand. "If he breaks your heart again, both Shane and I will break him."

After Calvin's whole apology and confession, I don't think that'll happen. I returned to my desk. There was no way I could focus on work, I have a date with Calvin to get ready for. I collected my things and the arrangement, said goodbye to June and left. Tonight was going to be the start of something new, and I couldn't wait.

About the Author

Ivy Marie grew up an army brat. Moving every two or three years, and finally settling in Ottawa, Ontario, Canada. This is where her passion for writing began. With each new book, she dives deeper into her imagination.

She writes both Supernatural Romance, featuring werewolves and vampires, as well as Contemporary Romance. These stories are not just words on a page; they are reflections of her own personality and dreams.

When I'm not lost in the world of words, you'll find me in the kitchen, whipping up sweet treats, or at my table, piecing together puzzles. These quiet moments are always accompanied by a glass of wine or a can of beer, making them all the more enjoyable.

You can find so much more by Ivy Marie on her website: https://ivymarieauthor.com/

Connect

I really appreciate you reading my book! Here are my social media coordinates;

Facebook: www.facebook.com/IvysStolenHearts
Instagram: ivymariebooks
Blue Sky: @ivymarie-author.bsky.social
X: @IvyMarie_Books
Website: www.ivymarieauthor.com

Don't forget about my wonderful cover artist - Shawna Russ;

Instagram: shawncolourart

Also By

Keep an eye out other books by Ivy Marie.

Like Hell this is Real (Book 1)

Like Hell this is Normal (Book 2)

Like Hell this is Happening (Book 3)

Like Hell Alternative (Alternate Reality)

www.ingramcontent.com/pod-product-compliance
Lightning Source LLC
Chambersburg PA
CBHW060229180626
46813CB00007B/3017